A Penny Blood Adventur

The New Dark Age

Other Penny Blood Adventures

- The Dark Nun's Church
- Maria Laveau's Army
- The Werewolves of London
- The Thirteenth Hour
- The Mad Lab
- Krampus
- Midwinter Vampires
- Walk the Plank
- The Leprechaun's Trap
- The New Dark Age

Mutanti Cycle

- Whispers of War: Part 1
- Tears of War: Part 1
- Lords of War: Part 1

A Penny Blood Adventure

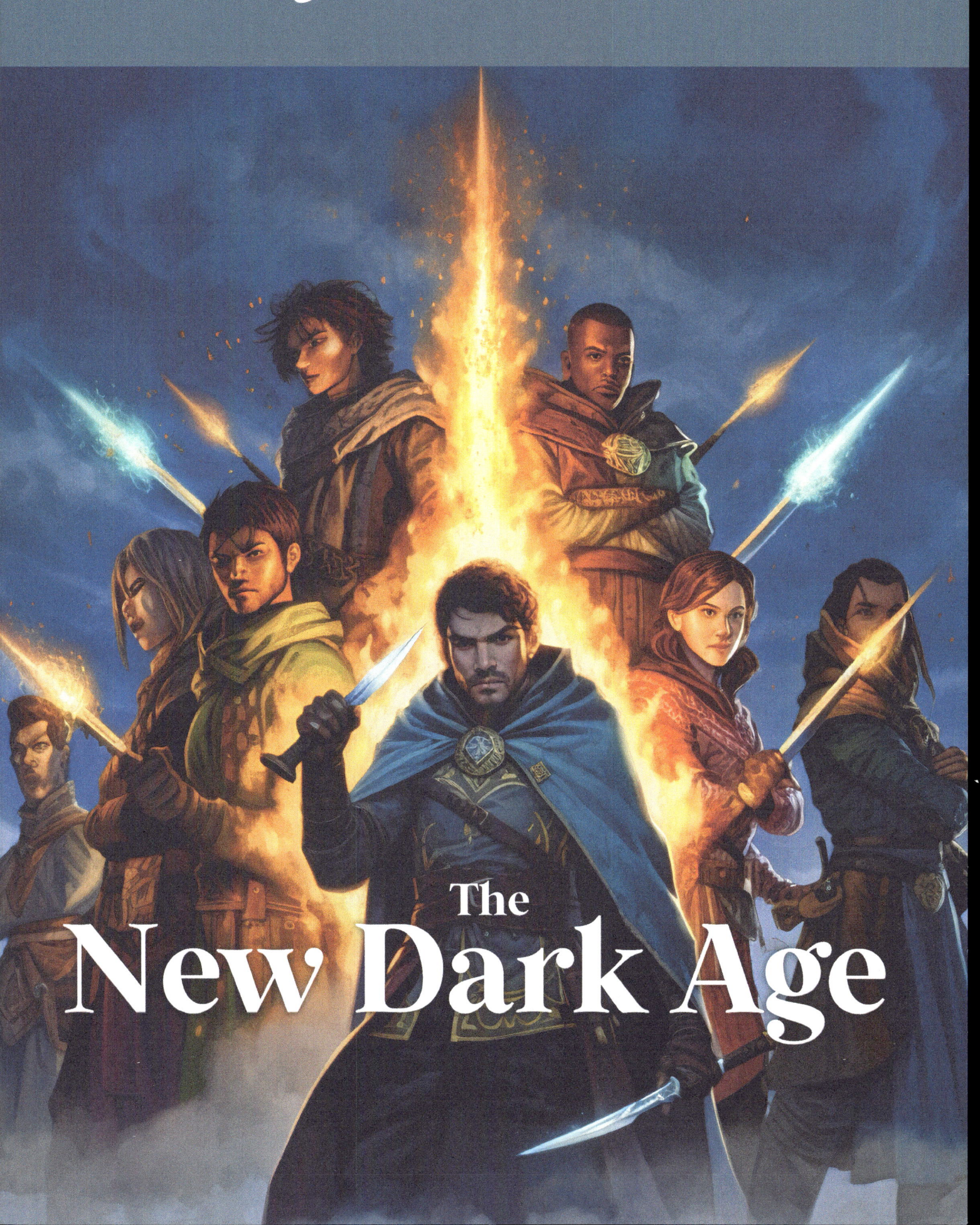

The New Dark Age

The New Dark Age

Running the Adventure 7
Structure for Each Encounter 7

The Shatterborn Class 9
The Shatterborn 9
Shatterborn Subclasses 9
Background: The Shatterborn 9
Quick Build 9
Shatterborn Class Table 11
The Shatterborn Class Features 11
Path of the Riftblade 13
Path of the Shaper 13
Path of the Wanderer 14
Challenges when playing a Shatterborn Class 14

History 16
The Time Before The Shattering 16
The Shattering 16
The Rise of The Iron Conclave 16

Starting the Adventure 18

The Broken Spire 20
The Iron Conclave Outpost 21
The Resistance Camp 22
The Cursed Entrance 24
The Crumbling Courtyard 25
Archmage's Quarters 26
The Lost Library 27
The Hall of Mirrors 29
The Warped Laboratory 31
The Echo Chamber 33
The Broken Spire 35

The Undercity 38
The Undercity Entrance 39
The Shadowed Alcoves 40
The Veilway 43
Labyrinthine Depths 45
Ethereal Glade 46
The Vault 48
The Iron Gate 49
The Undercity Market 51

Iron Conclave Fortress 59
The Guardhouse 59
The Courtyard 61
The War Room 62
Fortress Walls 63
The Shatter Room 63
Ritual Chamber 65

Resolution 67
Destruction of Magic (Iron Conclave Victory) 67
Preservation of Magic (Resistance Victory) 67
Balance (Compromise) 68
Magic Chaos (Failure) 68

Random Encounters 70

Scaling Monsters 71
Brute and Elite Creatures 71

Monsters 73
Arcane Echo 73
Conclave Guard 73
Conclave Guard (Brute) 74
Conclave Executioner 75
Echo Hound 75
Iron Wraith 76
Nexus Wisp 77
Prohibition Construct 78
Reclaimed Dead 79
Rune Golem 79
Shatterbeast 81
The Shattered 81
The Unraveled 82

Magic Items 85
Riftblade 85
Cloak of the Wandering Woods 85
Nexus Locket 85
Gloves of the Unraveled 85
Iron Conclave Sigil 85
Rift Shard 85

Spells 87
Shatter Spark 87

- Rift Blink 87
- Shape Matter 87
- Energy Cascade 87
- Reform 87
- Chaotic Shield 87
- Leviathan's Grasp 88
- Rift Storm 88
- Shatter Whisper 89
- Echoes of the Shattered 89
- Mist of the Wandering Woods 89
- Leviathan's Strength 89
- Nexus Pulse 89
- Shroud of the Unraveled 89

Non-Player Characters 91
- Iron Conclave 91
- Underground Resistance 91
- Neutral/Other NPCs 91

Mazes 93
- Complex Maze 93
- Complex Maze (solution) 94
- Simple Maze 95
- Simple Maze (solution) 96

Game within a Game 98
- Coin of Fates 98

Food and Fuel 100
- Shatterbeast Jerky (Snack) 100
- Iron Conclave Stew (Meal) 100
- Underground Resistance Mushroom Soup (Meal) 100
- Shattered Elixir (Non-Alcoholic Drink) 100
- Rift Shard Cocktail (Alcoholic Drink) 101

Maps 103
- The Broken Spire 103
- The Undercity 104
- The Iron Conclave Fortress 105

Special Thanks 106

Credits 107

Running the Adventure

Running the Adventure

Step into a world torn apart by the fear and distrust of magic. Will you fight to restore the arcane or will you forge a path in a world without magic? Your choice determines the fate in this immersive D&D 5e campaign.

In the wake of a catastrophic event known as The Shattering, magic has become unstable and dangerous, leading to its prohibition. The world has descended into a dark age where magic-users are hunted and feared. As magic fades, society teeters on the brink of a new era - an era that could either witness the resurgence of magic or its ultimate death.

"The New Dark Age" is a D&D 5th Edition campaign set in this world of dread and mystery. As players, you have the power to shape the destiny of this world. Will you join the Iron Conclave and ensure the death of magic for the safety of the world, or will you side with the Underground Resistance to reclaim the lost arcane arts?

Structure for Each Encounter

To help GMs manage the game, each encounter is split into the following sections:

- Encounter Name
- DM Information (to give you a summary of the encounter)
- Read Aloud
- Additional information (which gives you more detailed information and instructions on how to reconcile the encounter)
- Storyline
- Activity is meant as a fun, game-within-a-game section and is typically puzzles or games for the players.
- Monster and/or NPC (It tells you about any monster or NPC the players may meet in the encounter.)
- Lair Actions
- Reward (is what everyone is working towards!)

Encounters will often have information that is available later in the book. For instance, the details of a monster can be found in the Monster section.

Characters can choose to align themselves with either the Iron Conclave or the Underground Resistance. Each encounter has additional rules depending on which group you align with.

Lair Actions have been added to each encounter. Lair Actions can add a level of complexity triggered by the environment. This is a great way to challenge advanced characters.

The game is modular in design, allowing the GM to swap in and out content from other games. If you want to avoid using one of the monsters included in this campaign, swap it out with a different monster.

The structure for this and all Penny Blood Adventurers is to give you a framework you can easily work within and modify as the GM.

Shatterborn Class

The Shatterborn Class

The Shatterborn

"When The Shattering occurred, it was not only our world that was broken. Those of us who survived, who became Shatterborn... we carry that fracture within us. But in that rupture between what was and what is, there's power. Power to mend, power to break, power to shape our fate and the fate of this fractured world." – Ancient Lirael

In the aftermath of The Shattering, a few rare individuals found themselves uniquely touched by the catastrophe. These survivors, known as the Shatterborn, were imbued with the raw, chaotic magic unleashed during the world-altering event. This power, though unpredictable and dangerous, has the potential to reshape reality. As a Shatterborn, you are one of the few beings capable of harnessing and directing the untamed magical energies that now permeate the world.

Shatterborn have an unstable and sometimes volatile relationship with the chaotic magic within them. Each time they channel this power, they risk losing control and causing unintended harm, yet it is this very risk that can make them powerful allies in the new, dark age. To be a Shatterborn is to walk a knife's edge between control and chaos, but those who master this balance can change the fate of the world.

Shatterborn Subclasses

Path of the Riftblade

Shatterborn who walk the Path of the Riftblade become deadly conduits of chaotic magic, channeling the volatile energies into devastating arcane weaponry. A Riftblade is a fearsome opponent in battle, capable of manifesting shimmering blades, pulsating shields, and even armor crafted from raw, unpredictable energy. As masters of offensive and defensive magic, Riftblades are equally comfortable on the front lines as they are providing magical support to their allies.

Path of the Shaper

Shapers are Shatterborn who have dedicated themselves to understanding and controlling the chaotic magic of The Shattering. These powerful spellcasters manipulate the raw magic within them and the world around them with startling versatility. A Shaper might reshape the unstable energies to mend wounds, create protective barriers, or weave destructive spells. Despite the inherent risks, Shapers stand as a testament to the potential of their kind, proving that even the most volatile magic can be tamed.

Path of the Wanderer

Wanderers represent Shatterborn who have embraced their connection with the post-Shattering world. They are explorers, scouts, and survivalists, blending their chaotic magic with the environment around them. A Wanderer might use their power to communicate with Shatterbeasts, pass through a Rift unscathed, or manipulate the landscape to their advantage. With the world as their ally, Wanderers can adapt to almost any situation and are essential members of any adventuring party.

Background: The Shatterborn

Your life before The Shattering might be a distant memory, a hazy dream, or a forgotten past. The magic coursing through your veins has marked you, changed you, and made you a beacon of hope or a target of fear in this new world. Some view the Shatterborn with awe and reverence, seeing them as saviors who can restore the world. Others see them with suspicion and fear, regarding them as ticking time bombs ready to unleash another Shattering.

As a Shatterborn, your life is a constant struggle between understanding and controlling your powers, and dealing with a world that may not understand you. Your powers as a Shatterborn was gifted to you when The Shattering occurred. This means that your you now have the skills of your previous life, which may have been a warrior, scholar or any other profession and now you have been imbued with Shatterborn skills. This will be seen as a blessing for some but for others, the new skills will be perceived as a curse. Since The Shattering, there have been occasional small, localized mini-shatterings. The outcome of which means that any character can be infused with Shattering class options. Your path may be challenging, but it's also one of great potential. In this New Dark Age, your power could light the way forward.

Quick Build

When creating a Shatterborn character, you can follow these quick build recommendations:

Ability Scores: Start by putting your highest ability score in Constitution, this represents your character's physical resilience as a survivor of the Shattering. Next, if you plan on taking the Path of the Riftblade, prioritize Strength next as your combat abilities will rely on it. If you're planning on Path of the Shaper or Path of the Wanderer, prioritize Intelligence as your spellcasting abilities will rely on it. Your third-highest score should typically go into Wisdom to represent your mental fortitude and perception.

Race: Choose a race that enhances your key ability scores. For a Riftblade, a race like the Half-Orc or Dragonborn could be beneficial for their Strength bonus. For a Shaper or Wanderer, races like the High Elf or Gnome could be beneficial for their Intelligence bonus. Humans are also a good choice for any path due to their flexible ability score increases.

Background: The Shatterborn can come from any background, but consider the implications of your choice in light of the world's lore. A Sage or Hermit might have been studying magic when the Shattering happened, while a Soldier or City Watch might have been in the thick of the chaos when it occurred.

Class Equipment: As for class equipment, if you're going the route of the Riftblade, a melee weapon like a longsword or warhammer can be fitting. Shapers and Wanderers should start with a simple weapon like a staff that can also be used as an arcane focus.

Spells: Choose spells that fit your character's backstory and the way they survived the Shattering. A character who relied on stealth might choose spells like "Misty Step" or "Invisibility", while one who had to fight might choose "Shield" or "Magic Missile".

Remember, the most important part of character creation is creating a character you're excited to play, so don't feel like you need to strictly adhere to these suggestions!

Shatterborn Class Table

Keep in mind that as a hybrid class, the Shatterborn doesn't gain access to high-level spells as quickly as full spellcasters (such as wizards or clerics) but faster than half-casters (like rangers or paladins). Their spell progression should follow the pace of their class story and balance out with their other class features.

The spells available to a Shatterborn should be primarily defensive and utility in nature, reflecting their nature as survivors of the Shattering.

Level	Proficiency Bonus	Cantrips Known	1st	2nd	3rd	4th	5th	6th	7th	8th	9th
1	2	2	2	—	—	—	—	—	—	—	—
2	2	2	3	—	—	—	—	—	—	—	—
3	2	2	4	2	—	—	—	—	—	—	—
4	2	3	4	3	—	—	—	—	—	—	—
5	3	3	4	3	2	—	—	—	—	—	—
6	3	3	4	3	3	—	—	—	—	—	—
7	3	3	4	3	3	1	—	—	—	—	—
8	3	3	4	3	3	2	—	—	—	—	—
9	4	3	4	3	3	3	1	—	—	—	—
10	4	4	4	3	3	3	2	—	—	—	—
11	4	4	4	3	3	3	2	1	—	—	—
12	4	4	4	3	3	3	2	1	—	—	—
13	5	4	4	3	3	3	2	1	1	—	—
14	5	4	4	3	3	3	2	1	1	—	—
15	5	4	4	3	3	3	2	1	1	1	—
16	5	4	4	3	3	3	2	1	1	1	—
17	6	4	4	3	3	2	1	1	1	1	
18	6	4	4	3	3	3	1	1	1	1	
19	6	4	4	3	3	3	2	1	1	1	
20	6	4	4	3	3	3	3	2	2	1	1

The Shatterborn Class Features

Hit Points

Hit Dice: 1d8 per Shatterborn level

Hit Points at 1st Level: 8 + your Constitution modifier

Hit Points at Higher Levels: 1d8 (or 5) + your Constitution modifier per Shatterborn level after 1st

Proficiencies

Armor: Light armor

Weapons: Simple weapons

Tools: None

Saving Throws: Constitution, Intelligence

Skills: Choose two from Arcana, History, Insight, Perception, Persuasion, and Survival

Starting Equipment

You start with the following equipment, in addition to the equipment granted by your background:

- (a) a martial weapon (Riftblade only) or (b) two simple weapons
- (a) a dungeoneer's pack or (b) an explorer's pack
- Leather armor and an arcane focus

Level 1: Shattering Touch

You can channel the Shattering's raw energy through your touch. As an action, you can touch a nonmagical item and shatter it into pieces. The item must be a handheld object no larger than a 5-foot cube. This can also be used as a melee spell attack against a creature, dealing 1d8 force damage.

Level 2: Shatterborn Path

At 2nd level, you choose the path you walk as a Shatterborn: Path of the Riftblade, Path of the Shaper, or Path of the Wanderer, all detailed at the end of the class description. Your path grants you features at 2nd level and again at 6th, 10th, 14th, and 18th level.

Level 3: Unstable Casting

Starting at 3rd level, whenever you cast a spell of 1st level or higher, you can choose to cast it as an Unstable spell. When you do so, roll a d20. On a 1, the spell backfires and affects you or a random target instead (DM's choice). On a 20, the spell effect is maximized (all dice rolls are treated as having rolled the maximum result). This feature embodies the volatile and unpredictable nature of Shatterborn magic.

Level 4: Ability Score Improvement

When you reach 4th level, and again at 8th, 12th, 16th, and 19th level, you can increase one ability score of your choice by 2, or you can increase two ability scores of your choice by 1. As normal, you can't increase an ability score above 20 using this feature.

Level 5: Shattering Resistance

Beginning at 5th level, your exposure to the chaotic magic of the Shattering has fortified your body. You gain resistance to force damage and advantage on saving throws against spells and other magical effects.

Level 6: Shatterborn Path feature

Level 7: Shattering Blast

Starting at 7th level, you can unleash a wave of Shattering energy as an action. Each creature in a 15-foot cone originating from you must make a Dexterity saving throw. On a failed save, a creature takes 3d8 force damage and is pushed 10 feet away from you. On a successful save, it takes half as much damage and isn't pushed. You can use this feature a number of times equal to your Constitution modifier (minimum of once), and you regain all expended uses when you finish a long rest.

Level 8: Ability Score Improvement

Level 9: Echoes of the Shattering

At 9th level, your link with the Shattering allows you to pull magical echoes from the past. You can cast the spell "augury" without expending a spell slot or material components. You can use this feature once per short or long rest.

Level 10: Shatterborn Path feature

Level 11: Unstable Evolution

Starting at 11th level, your body has further adapted to the Shattering's volatile magic. You gain one of the following features of your choice:

Evasion: When subjected to an effect that allows you to make a Dexterity saving throw to take only half damage, you instead take no damage if you succeed on the saving throw, and only half damage if you fail.

Arcane Sight: You can see the presence of magic within 60 feet of you. This works like the detect magic spell but isn't blocked by stone, wood, or other common materials. You can turn this ability on or off as an action.

Arcane Resistance: You gain resistance to damage from spells.

Level 12: Ability Score Improvement

Level 13: Shattering Presence

Beginning at 13th level, your very presence can disturb the flow of magic around you. As an action, you can force all creatures within 30 feet of you to make a Wisdom saving throw or be unable to cast spells until the end of your next turn. You can use this feature once per long rest.

Level 14: Shatterborn Path feature

Level 15: Overload

Starting at 15th level, when you score a critical hit with a melee attack, you can choose to overload the target with unstable magic. The target must make a Constitution saving throw against your spell save DC. On a failed save, the target is stunned until the end of its next turn. Once you use this feature, you can't use it again until you finish a short or long rest.

Level 16: Ability Score Improvement

Level 17: Shattering Burst

At 17th level, your Shattering Blast becomes even more potent. The range of the cone increases to 30 feet, the damage increases to 4d8, and creatures that failed their saves are pushed 20 feet away.

Level 18: Shatterborn Path feature

Level 19: Ability Score Improvement

Level 20: Avatar of the Shattering

At 20th level, you become a living conduit for the chaotic magic of the Shattering. As an action, you can undergo a transformation. For 1 minute, you gain the following benefits:

- At the start of each of your turns, you regain 10 hit points.
- Your Unstable Casting feature doesn't backfire. Instead, when you roll a 1 on an unstable spell cast, you can reroll the spell against a different target within range.
- When you are hit by an attack, you can use your reaction to release a burst of Shattering energy, dealing force damage equal to your level to the attacker.

Once you use this feature, you can't use it again until you finish a long rest.

Path of the Riftblade

Riftblades use the chaotic energy of the Shattering to enhance their physical capabilities and to weaponize the unstable magic. They are feared warriors, capable of tearing rifts in reality to devastate their foes.

Rift Strike (2nd Level)

You learn to infuse your weapon attacks with chaotic energy. Once per turn, when you hit a creature with a weapon attack, you can deal an additional 1d4 force damage. In addition, you gain proficiency in medium armor and martial weapons.

Rift Step (6th Level)

You can use the chaotic energy to twist space around you. As a bonus action, you can teleport to an unoccupied space you can see within 30 feet. You can use this feature a number of times equal to your Charisma modifier (minimum of once), and you regain all expended uses when you finish a long rest.

Riftblade's Resilience (10th Level)

Your constant exposure to chaotic magic fortifies your body. You gain resistance to two types of damage of your choice: acid, cold, fire, lightning, or thunder.

Reality Slash (14th Level)

You can create a dangerous rift in reality with a swing of your weapon. As an action, you make a melee attack against a creature. On a hit, the creature takes an extra 4d10 force damage, and each creature within 5 feet of it must succeed on a Dexterity saving throw or take 2d10 force damage.

Master of the Rift (18th Level)

Your mastery over rifts reaches its zenith. When you take the Attack action on your turn, you can teleport up to 30 feet before each attack once every 5 rounds. You must finish a short or long rest before you can use this feature again.

Path of the Shaper

Shapers use their connection to the Shattering to influence and reshape reality. They are adept at manipulating unstable magic for a variety of effects, and are sought after for their abilities.

Reality Weave (2nd Level)

You can reshape reality to mimic certain spells. You can cast "minor illusion" and "mage hand" at will, without using a spell slot.

Shaper's Ward (6th Level)

When you or a creature within 30 feet of you is hit by an attack, you can use your reaction to grant a +5 bonus to the target's AC, potentially causing the attack to miss.

Reality Bend (10th Level)

You gain the ability to bend reality to your will. As an action, you can force a creature you can see within 60 feet of you to make a Wisdom saving throw. On a failed save, you can move the creature up to 30 feet in any direction.

Shaper's Refuge (14th Level)

As an action, you can reshape the surrounding area to create a protective sphere. For 1 minute, you and your allies gain half cover while inside the sphere. You must finish a short or long rest before you can use this feature again.

Master of Shapes (18th Level)

Your reality shaping abilities reach their pinnacle. As an action, you can choose a point you can see within 60 feet of you. You reshape reality in a 20-foot-radius sphere centered on that point for a five-minute period of time. You can create any of the following effects within the sphere:

- Create a zone of difficult terrain where enemies must roll with disadvantage.

- Grant up to six creatures of your choice the ability to fly up to 20 ft in distance.
- Replicate the effects of the "Wall of Force" spell.

Each effect only lasts within the field of influence and time you have the sphere generated.

Path of the Wanderer

Wanderers use their connection with the Shattering to adapt and survive in any environment. They are hardy explorers, often the first to venture into areas where the magical effect of The Shattering is unstable.

Shattered Survival (2nd Level)

You gain proficiency in the Survival skill, and you can navigate any Shattered area as if you had a map. You also gain advantage on saving throws against the effects of unstable magic.

Chaotic Adaptation (6th Level)

Your body adapts to thrive in the harshest environments. You gain resistance to cold and fire damage, and you don't suffer the effects of extreme heat or cold.

Reality Compass (10th Level)

As an action, you can sense the direction to the nearest significant source of unstable magic. You can also determine whether any creatures are affected by unstable magic within 60 feet of you.

Shattered Walk (14th Level)

You have learned to use the Shattering to move through the world in unexpected ways. As a bonus action, you can step into a Shattered space and reappear in another Shattered space you can see within 60 feet.

Master of the Wandering (18th Level)

Your connection to the Shattering allows you to manipulate the chaotic magic to protect you and your allies. As an action, you can create a shimmering field around yourself and up to five creatures of your choice within 30 feet of you. For 1 minute, you and the chosen creatures gain resistance to all damage. You must finish a long rest before you can use this feature again.

Challenges when playing a Shatterborn Class

Being a Shatterborn certainly brings a unique set of challenges and difficulties, a reflection of their profound connection to the magic that was disrupted during the Shattering. Here are some potential drawbacks:

Unstable Magic: Shatterborn magic is inherently unpredictable. While this can sometimes result in extraordinary displays of power, it can also lead to dangerous magical backfires or unexpected effects.

Social Stigma: Given that the Shattering was a catastrophic magical event, many people harbor fear and distrust of any magic users, including Shatterborn. In some places, Shatterborn might be outcasts or be forced to hide their abilities to avoid persecution.

The Iron Conclave: As the Shatterborn are living proof that magic still exists and can be harnessed, they are a primary target of the Iron Conclave. Being pursued by such a relentless and powerful organization can put a Shatterborn and their allies in constant danger.

Psychological Struggles: The traumatic experiences surrounding the Shattering may have left deep psychological scars. Shatterborn may struggle with feelings of guilt, nightmares, and the challenge of controlling their unstable magical powers.

Physical Strain: Manipulating the volatile post-Shattering magic puts a strain on the Shatterborn's body. This might manifest as physical fatigue, unexpected illness, or even temporary loss of magical abilities after heavy usage.

Magical Anomalies: The Shatterborn are intrinsically linked with the magical forces disrupted during the Shattering. As such, they might attract magical phenomena or creatures, resulting in an increased likelihood of dangerous encounters.

Remember, these negatives can also offer interesting roleplay opportunities and plot hooks for your campaign. While they present challenges, they also provide depth and complexity to Shatterborn characters.

History

History

The Time Before The Shattering

The era preceding The Shattering was known as the Age of Arcana, a golden age of prosperity, enlightenment, and magic. Magic was as commonplace as technology is today, integrated into every aspect of life, from healing to transportation, from communication to defense. Kingdoms were governed by councils of powerful mages, and arcane universities trained new generations of magic users.

Non-magical skills and crafts weren't entirely forgotten, but they were often considered secondary to magical aptitude. There was a social divide, with magic users holding most of the power and prestige.

The Shattering

The Shattering was triggered by an experiment gone horribly wrong. A group of the most powerful Archmages attempted a ritual to tap directly into the raw source of magic, hoping to ascend to a near-godlike state and bring about a new era of magical evolution.

However, the ritual spiraled out of control, causing a catastrophic explosion of raw magical energy that tore through the fabric of reality. The resulting shockwave rippled across the entire world, disrupting the flow of magic and causing catastrophic, unpredictable effects.

This event was the most devastating disaster in history, causing widespread destruction and death. Magic, once a tool for prosperity and comfort, became unstable, unpredictable, and often deadly.

The Rise of The Iron Conclave

It has been a decade since The Shattering. Magic is no longer reliable, and those who use it are viewed with fear and suspicion. In this chaos, a group of non-magic users seized the opportunity to restore order.

Calling themselves the Iron Conclave, they blamed the unchecked use of magic for the disaster and called for a return to a pre-magical society. Their message resonated with a traumatized population, and they rapidly gained power.

The Iron Conclave implemented strict measures against the use of magic and began a campaign to hunt down magic users, seeing them as potential threats. They confiscated and secured magical artifacts, aiming to prevent any chance of another Shattering.

Their rule is harsh but brought a sense of stability and order. Many people, particularly those who had suffered during The Shattering, supported them. However, not everyone agreed with their hardline stance, leading to the formation of the Underground Resistance.

Staring the Adventure

Starting the Adventure

The skies above cracked open, a surge of pure, untamed magic spilling forth from a rift, a cataclysmic event that would come to be known as The Shattering. Uncontrolled energy exploded across the realm, bringing forth destruction and change in equal measures. The reality of the world as it was known was being irrevocably altered.

Commander Gaius Tarn stood amidst the chaos, his city, his home, and his family, all dissolving under the terrifying power of the unleashed magic. He fell to his knees, his fists clenched tight as his voice echoed in a tortured scream. This devastation, the price of hubris, was a sharp lesson for humanity's blind trifling with powers beyond their grasp. From this despair, the Iron Conclave was born, a group determined to stamp out the volatile and destructive force of magic.

Simultaneously, deep in the clandestine tunnels of the city, the last of the magic users went quickly into hiding. Elandra, then a young sorceress, watched the rift above widen with terror and awe. She whispered to her companion, Therin the Swift, "It's happening." His eyes darted around their shelter, his survival instincts sparking. "We need to get the others to safety." And they did. From the catastrophe of The Shattering, the Underground Resistance emerged, a beacon of hope for those who believed magic was not the enemy, but a friend who had lost its way.

In the grand study of her sanctum, Ancient Lirael, a respected Archmage before The Shattering, saw the world being torn apart. The shock on her face was replaced by resignation. "So this is it," she murmured, "the price of our folly."

The city crumbled around Inquisitor Drava, her hardened eyes meeting those of Blacksmith Albern. Her words rang clear, despite the chaos. "We've got to do something, Albern." He nodded, his grip on his hammer firming. They were the hands that built the Iron Conclave, a hammer to strike down the wild magic running amok.

In the distant Wandering Woods, Ranger Yoren saw his world transform. He knew he would adapt, just as nature would. Simultaneously, within the quiet solitude of the Lost Library, Curator Marvus found himself surrounded by the end of the world within the pages of his beloved books. These artifacts of the old world would light the path in the dark age to come.

At the Broken Spire, the Ghost of Quillara the Riftweaver observed the world's descent into chaos with a spectral heart filled with sorrow. From her ruined tower, she saw her world join her in her spectral state. Yet, amidst all the despair, a seed of hope took root.

From the ashes of The Shattering arose a new world, a realm of mystery and danger, of despair and hope. In the heart of this destruction, two forces were born, the Iron Conclave, sworn to eradicate the source of their pain, and the Underground Resistance, seeking to restore harmony between magic and mankind.

The age of magic is over. The New Dark Age has begun.

The Iron Conclave, comprised of those scarred by The Shattering, seeks to eradicate magic, seeing it as too dangerous to be controlled. They believe the only way to prevent another cataclysm is to drain magic from the world entirely. Conversely, the Underground Resistance sees magic as a part of their identity, a gift to be harnessed and stabilized. They fight for a world where magic is rebalanced and restored, where its misuse is controlled.

The party has arrived at The Broken Spire under the looming shadow of this conflict. Maybe they've been sent by a distant lord who has interests in the outcome, or perhaps they have personal stakes in this fight. Each of the characters must decide their allegiance. Will they stand with the Iron Conclave, the Underground Resistance, or remain neutral, attempting to carve their own path amidst the chaos?

The Broken Spire

The Broken Spire

The Broken Spire is a location of pivotal importance in your campaign, embodying both the historical and current struggle for magic in this New Dark Age. Before The Shattering caused the spire to break, it was known as the Arcane Pinnacle. The name emphasized the Spire's status as the pinnacle of magical learning and research. It symbolized a peak of achievement and ambition that magic practitioners aspired to reach.

Here are some key points to consider when introducing this location to your players:

Symbol of Power: The Broken Spire is a stark reminder of a time when magic was a force to be reckoned with. Its cracked, jagged silhouette reaches skyward, a testament to a devastating event, The Shattering. Use this symbolism to convey the gravity of what was lost and the deep-rooted fear of magic that pervades society.

Stronghold of the Iron Conclave: Now serving as a stronghold for the Iron Conclave, the Broken Spire represents their power and resolve. This should be evident in the patrols of soldiers, the fortified defenses, and the general atmosphere of control and surveillance.

Layered Encounters: The Spire, with its numerous levels and rooms, provides a plethora of opportunities for varied encounters. The Echo Chamber, Archmage's Quarters, Warped Laboratory, and other sections each come with their distinct challenges and rewards. Remember to design these encounters to reflect the shifting nature of the Spire, with elements of its magical past clashing with the militaristic present.

Dangers and Secrets: As a place where magic once flourished, the Broken Spire is still teeming with latent magic, trapped creatures, and hazardous areas. In addition, its past as a place of magical learning means there are many secrets yet to be discovered—hidden chambers, forgotten artifacts, and arcane knowledge.

Dynamic Environments: The Spire is a blend of the stable and the unpredictable. While the Iron Conclave has attempted to impose order, echoes of the Spire's magical past can cause sudden and dramatic changes—surges of arcane energy, rooms that disobey the laws of physics, and more. Use these to create an environment of suspense and unpredictability.

Strategic Importance: The Broken Spire is a critical location for both the Iron Conclave and the Underground Resistance. For the Conclave, it is a symbol of their dominance and control, a base of operations, and a place to house and study confiscated magical artifacts. For the Resistance, it is a target for their efforts to restore magic—a place to rescue captive magic users, retrieve important artifacts, and potentially discover the means to restore magic to the world.

The Broken Spire is a location that brings together the themes and conflicts of your campaign. Use it to challenge your players, to engage them with the deeper narrative, and to pose questions that make them think about their characters' views on magic, power, and the nature of the world they inhabit.

In the heart of the woods, a haunting silhouette pierces the horizon: the Broken Spire. Once a grand testament to the power of magic and the intellectual prowess of its former masters, the Archmages, it now stands as a grim monument to the Shattering.

Its mighty stone towers, intricately adorned with arcane symbols, are sundered and twisted, a testament to the cataclysmic forces that tore through this place. The once vibrant gardens are now a tangled mess of thorny vines and petrified trees, a somber reflection of the grandeur that has been lost. Yet amidst the ruin and decay, an eerie beauty persists, as if the Spire itself refuses to forget its past glory.

This once magnificent seat of magical learning is now a labyrinth of distorted passages and crumbling chambers. Magical energy crackles in the air, wild and unpredictable, warping reality in its vicinity. It's a place where the past is trapped like a ghost, echoing through the silent halls.

Many are drawn to the Broken Spire, captivated by its mystery and the promise of hidden knowledge and power. Adventurers and scholars alike delve into its treacherous depths, braving the roaming Shatterbeasts, lingering Arcane Echoes, and the ever-present threat of the Spire's unstable magic.

Despite the dangers, the Broken Spire remains a place of significance for many. For the Iron Conclave, it's a potent symbol of the danger of unregulated magic, and they have claimed it as a strategic outpost in their crusade against magic users. For the Underground Resistance, it represents hope, a beacon from a time when magic flourished, and they believe that the Spire holds the key to reclaiming that lost era. For both groups, it is the unstable magic held within the Rift Shard that will deliver a new future. Secrets of the Rift Shard are located throughout the Broken Spire.

The Broken Spire is not simply a remnant of the past; it is a battleground for the future, a place where the destiny of magic in this New Dark Age will be decided. It is here, amidst the echoes of past glory and the rumblings of future conflicts, that heroes will rise, destinies will be forged, and the fate of the world will be forever altered.

The characters can explore the Broken Spire to find information on the Rift Shard with the goal to either permanently destroy magic or stabilize magic so it can be used safely. The characters can also visit camps for either the Iron Conclave or the Underground Resistance and complete the following tasks before moving to the next location, the Undercity.

Throughout their missions, the party will face various encounters and challenges, such as engaging in combat with Iron Conclave soldiers and magical creatures, solving arcane puzzles, navigating through a labyrinth of shifting corridors, dealing with various magical and mechanical traps, and interacting with different entities within the Broken Spire. The outcomes of their actions and choices would further shape their journey in this New Dark Age.

The Iron Conclave Outpost

A fortified encampment near the Spire, housing a contingent of Iron Wraiths. It's heavily guarded and frequently patrolled, but it might also contain valuable intelligence on the Conclave's operations. An NPC for the Iron Conclave, Inquisitor Drava, is also at this location.

The building is a stark and imposing fortification made from sturdy dark stone and metal. The architecture is harsh and utilitarian, with high walls studded with guard towers. Bright torches illuminate the outpost, casting long, flickering shadows. The area around the outpost is cleared of any cover, ensuring that approaching intruders can be easily spotted.

This encounter is centered around the Iron Conclave Outpost, a fortified position near the Spire. This location provides a lot of opportunities for intrigue, stealth, and combat, depending on how your party wants to handle it. There are also opportunities for tense social interactions with Inquisitor Drava, a powerful figure in the Iron Conclave. The Iron Wraiths serve as powerful and intimidating guards that can provide a challenging combat encounter.

Characters Aligned to Iron Conclave

As members of the Iron Conclave, the Characters will receive their assignments from Inquisitor Drava. She is a harsh but fair commander, expecting absolute obedience and discipline from her subordinates. The assignments she gives to the Characters reflect the Conclave's main objective: eradicating magic and any threats it poses. The Characters are expected to investigate the magical surge, neutralize a dangerous artifact, and capture a Resistance spy, all while maintaining their cover within the Outpost.

Characters Aligned to Underground Resistance

For Characters aligned with the Underground Resistance, the Outpost provides a wealth of opportunities. They could gather valuable intelligence on the Conclave's operations, sabotage their efforts, or even attempt to convert some of the lower-ranking Conclave members to their cause. However, they will need to be careful and stealthy, as the Outpost is heavily guarded by Iron Wraiths and patrolled regularly by Inquisitor Drava herself.

Iron Conclave Tasks

Inquisitor Drava can be approached and she can share the following tasks for the Iron Conclave:

Magical Surge Investigation

Drava has been closely monitoring the Broken Spire for any signs of magical activity. A recent surge has caught her attention, and she wants the Characters to investigate. She provides them with a device that can track and analyze magical energy, which they must use to pinpoint the source of the surge. Once the source is located, the Characters are to neutralize it by any means necessary. This could lead them to an unexpected magical creature, an artifact, or perhaps a hidden enclave of the Underground Resistance.

Artifact Destruction

The Iron Conclave has intercepted information suggesting that a powerful magical artifact, potentially dangerous if left unchecked, is hidden within the Broken Spire. Drava instructs the Characters to find the artifact and neutralize it. This could involve destroying the artifact, a process that may require solving riddles, breaking curses, or even battling a guardian creature. Alternatively, if destruction proves too risky or impossible, they should confiscate the artifact and return it to the Iron Conclave for containment and study.

Spy Hunt

A spy for the Underground Resistance has infiltrated the region, and Drava believes the spy is hiding somewhere within or near the Broken Spire. The spy is **Therin the Swift.** She provides the Characters with a description and name of the spy, though these might be aliases or decoys. The spy is believed to be carrying critical information about the Iron Conclave's plans and must be captured before they can deliver this information to the Resistance. This mission could involve tracking, interrogation, and a tense game of cat-and-mouse as the Characters try to find the spy before they slip away.

Completing the Tasks

If the characters are aligned to the Iron Conclave, then Inquisitor Drava will ask them to visit the Undercity and disrupt the Underground Resistance before finally going to the Iron Conclave Fortress. As the DM, you can choose how many tasks need to be completed before sending the characters to the Undercity.

Finding the Iron Conclave Sigil

The Iron Conclave Sigil, an item of importance within the Iron Conclave, is not casually discarded. Discovering one in the Outpost requires effort and cunning from the Characters. Here are a few possibilities:

Through a thorough search: Characters could discover the Sigil while exploring the outpost, looking for resources or intelligence. Encourage an Investigation check (DC 15). Success unveils the Sigil camouflaged amidst other items, perhaps in an officer's quarters or a well-secured chest. In case the Sigil is in a locked compartment, a Dexterity check with proficiency if using thieves' tools (DC 15) is needed to unlock and access it.

Through pickpocketing: Should Characters manage to get within personal space of high-ranking Iron Conclave members, such as Inquisitor Drava, a successful Sleight of Hand check (DC 15) allows them to subtly swipe the Sigil. Note that if caught in the act, this could lead to immediate escalation, resulting in combat or a high stakes chase.

Through diplomacy or deception: If the Characters are covertly infiltrating the Iron Conclave or have convinced a Conclave member of their loyalty, they may be offered the Sigil as a token of trust or gratitude for completed tasks. This might necessitate successful Charisma (Persuasion or Deception) checks, with the DC varying depending on the NPC's disposition and the believability of the PC's story, though a typical DC might be 15.

Through combat: If a battle occurs and the Characters triumph over an Iron Wraith or another high-ranking Conclave member, they could retrieve the Sigil from the fallen foe's belongings.

Remember, possessing an Iron Conclave Sigil can have intriguing social consequences. While it might grant access within the Conclave, it could also attract unwanted suspicion or direct confrontation.

Lair Actions

On initiative count 20 (losing initiative ties), Inquisitor Drava can use one of the following Lair Actions:

Alarm Bells: Drava orders the guards to sound the alarm, alerting 1d4 Iron Wraith within the Outpost.

Fortify Defenses: Drava bolsters the Outpost's defenses with 1d4 Iron Wraiths, causing iron gates to fall and block off certain areas. The Characters will need to find alternate routes or attempt to lift the heavy gates.

Anti-Magic Surge: Drava triggers an anti-magic device within the Outpost, causing a wave of anti-magic energy to spread out. For one round, all magic use within a 60-foot radius of the device is suppressed.

Remember to maintain a tense and challenging atmosphere throughout this encounter. The Iron Conclave is a dangerous and resourceful enemy, and they will use every tool at their disposal to stop the Characters' progress.

Monster

Iron Wraith

NPC

Inquisitor Drava

Reward

Iron Conclave Sigil

The Resistance Camp

A hidden camp in the wilderness around the Spire, where members of the Resistance gather and plan their actions. They are wary of strangers but can become valuable allies if trust is earned.

The Resistance Camp is set in a clearing amidst a dense, ancient forest. Concealed by heavy foliage and clever illusions, it comes alive as you step through an invisible boundary. Small tents, patched together with various materials, are scattered around the clearing, interspersed with cooking fires and training grounds. Magic users huddle in groups, sharing knowledge and honing their skills, while others mend gear or study maps and intelligence reports. A sense of quiet determination permeates the camp. Underneath the canopy, a group of rogues practices stealth techniques, and the air is filled with the soft whispers of spell incantations and the occasional laugh. At the center of the camp, a majestic old tree stands, its trunk etched with mystical symbols that glow softly, serving as the Resistance's clandestine emblem.

This encounter at the Resistance Camp is a great opportunity to add depth to your world and NPCs. Keep the tone secretive and tense, with the Resistance members initially distrustful of strangers. Characters like Therin the Swift can help bridge the gap, if they see potential in the Characters to aid their cause. Highlight the stakes and urgency of the tasks at hand and emphasize that secrecy and swift actions are key to their survival and the success of their operations. Depending on the alignment of your Characters, they may choose to betray the Resistance to the Iron Conclave or take up arms alongside them.

Characters Aligned to Iron Conclave

If your Characters are aligned with the Iron Conclave, this encounter could act as a turning point. They might choose to infiltrate the camp covertly, gather intelligence, and report back to Inquisitor Drava. Alternatively, they might see the Resistance's struggles firsthand and question their alliance with the Conclave.

Characters Aligned to Underground Resistance

If your Characters are aligned with the Resistance, they can become key players in the fight against the Iron Conclave. Therin's tasks could send them into the heart of danger, cementing their role as critical allies of the Resistance. They might strategize with the leaders, help train newer members, or participate in rescue missions and artifact hunts.

Underground Resistance Tasks

Therin the Swift has information on additional tasks the Characters can complete. They are:

Rescue Mission

Several members of the Resistance were captured during a reconnaissance mission near the Broken Spire. They are believed to be held in the Echo Chamber, a notorious prison known for amplifying the cries of prisoners and suppressing their magical abilities. The Characters must stealthily infiltrate the Broken Spire, locate the captives, and plan a rescue. Place an emphasis on the importance of discretion – if the Iron Conclave becomes aware of their presence, it could spell disaster. The Characters might use a variety of skills and abilities to bypass guards, including Deception, Stealth, or Illusion magic. The DM might call for a series of DC checks, such as DC 15 Stealth or Deception checks to bypass Conclave patrols or a DC 18 Dexterity check (using Thieves' Tools) to unlock the Echo Chamber.

Artifact Retrieval

Learned sage and historian Ancient Lirael has discovered references to a potent artifact known as the Nexus Locket. Believed to be hidden within the Archmage's Quarters in the Broken Spire, this artifact is rumored to have the power to stabilize magic in the surrounding area. The task is twofold - find the artifact before the Iron Conclave does and figure out how to activate it. This campaign might require numerous Arcana checks, such as a DC 18 Arcana check to decipher ancient texts or a DC 20 Investigation check to locate a hidden entrance to the Archmage's Quarters. Once found, understanding and activating the Nexus Locket might require additional DC 20 Arcana checks.

Securing the Experiments

Several highly sensitive magical experiments were left behind in the Warped Laboratory after the Shattering. Their unstable magical nature makes them invaluable to the Resistance for studying and potentially stabilizing magic. However, the experiments are delicate, and mishandling them could trigger unpredictable effects.

The party's task is to carefully retrieve as many of these experiments as they can and bring them back to the Resistance camp. For each experiment safely returned, the Resistance has pledged to reward the Characters with 50gp.

For the final task, Securing the Experiments, The Warped Laboratory is filled with strange, volatile magical energies. As the Characters explore the laboratory, call for DC 17 Investigation or Perception checks to find the experiments.

Each experiment is delicate. For each hour of travel, or any time the Characters engage in combat or other strenuous activity, call for a DC 15 Dexterity (Acrobatics) or a DC 15 Dexterity saving throw. On a failed save, and an experiment is dropped.

When an experiment is dropped, it triggers a magical effect. You can decide the effects, or use the Wild Magic Surge table (PHB p.104) for inspiration. Effects could range from harmless (such as everyone's hair standing on end) to dangerous (like a Fireball centered on the dropped vial).

This campaign adds a level of risk and tension as the Characters must not only navigate the dangerous lab but also handle volatile magical experiments while under potential threat from patrolling Iron Conclave forces. The promise of a tangible reward for each experiment provides a clear motivation for the Characters and a measure of their success.

Completing the Tasks

If the characters are aligned to the Underground Resistance, then Therin the Swift will ask them to visit the Undercity and support the Underground Resistance before finally going to the Iron Conclave Fortress where the Rift Shard can be found. As the DM, you can choose how many tasks need to be completed before sending the characters to the Undercity.

Lair Actions

The Resistance has fortified their camp with protective magic. On initiative count 20, losing all initiative ties, the Resistance Camp takes a lair action to cause one of the following magical effects:

The Camp triggers an illusion spell, causing the clearing to appear empty and untouched. Anyone inside the camp becomes invisible as long as they remain still.

A magic barrier springs up around the Camp, granting +2 to AC and saving throws to everyone inside the Camp until the next initiative count 20.

The Camp's central tree pulses with a wave of healing energy. Each creature of the Camp's choice in the camp regains 1d6 hit points.

NPC
Therin the Swift

The Cursed Entrance

This is the entrance to the Broken Spire, filled with runes and glyphs that are designed to ward off intruders. Some glyphs may hold curses, while others might offer protections or blessings to those who can understand them. The riddle etched into the stone monument serves as both the key to unlocking the entrance door, and as an eerie portent from ages past, a terrible omen predicting the Shattering and its prolonged impact.

Before you stands the entrance to the Broken Spire, a grand archway wrought from stone that seems to pulse with an unseen energy. Towering above you, the intricate array of glyphs and runes shimmer with ethereal light, their patterns woven into the very fabric of the stone. Some are faint and almost entirely worn away, while others glow brightly, pulsating in time with the heartbeat of the Spire. They form a hypnotic tableau, shifting and morphing even as you watch, each symbol seemingly alive and imbued with a potent arcane force. The ancient door sits heavily in its frame, undisturbed for the last decade, awaiting those who can correctly decipher its magical lock. Near the path to the archway sits a small stone monument, upon which is etched a mysterious message that reads:

"The watchful warden whispered his warning,

its message lost amidst the terrible shattering of every beacon.

The road to recovery is tortuous,

with hope the greatest guide to open possibility."

To unlock the door, the glyphs must be touched in the following sequence: Glyph of the Warden, Glyph of the Silent Whisper, Glyph of the Shattered Star, Glyph of the Wandering Path, and finally, Glyph of the Archmage's Key. Whenever each glyph is touched in the correct order, that glyph glows brightly as an indication of the correct choice. A successful DC 15 Intelligence (Arcana) check confirms the required method of a 5-glyph sequence to unlock the door, but not which glyphs or their order. This same check also reveals that the puzzle can be "reset" by everyone stepping at least 10 feet back from the door.

The Glyphs

Glyph of the Warden: A glyph shaped like a stylized eye. If touched, the glyph casts a DC 15 Wisdom saving throw. On a failed save, the character is afflicted by a magical compulsion to tell the truth for the next hour.

Glyph of the Shattered Star: This glyph looks like a star with a crack down the middle. If touched, it casts a minor illusion spell that makes the character believe they're being showered with sparks. This is more surprising than harmful and fades after a moment.

Glyph of the Silent Whisper: This glyph resembles a stylized ear. When activated, it silences all noise within a 10-foot radius for one minute, essentially casting a silence spell.

Glyph of the Wandering Path: This glyph depicts a meandering path. When touched, it casts confusion on the character who must succeed on a DC 15 Wisdom saving throw or be affected by the spell.

Glyph of the Archmage's Key: A complex glyph depicting a stylized key. This is the last glyph in the sequence to unlock the door. Touching this glyph without touching the previous glyphs in order casts a DC 15 Constitution saving throw. On a failed save, the character takes 2d10 psychic damage as their mind is overwhelmed with magical energy.

Glyph of the Howling Gale: This glyph depicts an abstract swirl, reminiscent of a fierce storm. When activated, the glyph emits a powerful gust of wind, strong enough to knock back intruders. It casts Gust of Wind (spell save DC 15) directly in front of it for up to 1 minute, centered on itself. Creatures in the line of the wind must succeed on a Strength saving throw or be pushed 15 feet away.

Glyph of the Iron Shell: This glyph appears to be a layered shell or perhaps an armadillo curling into a defensive position. When touched, it casts Shield of Faith on the creature that activated it, adding a +2 bonus to their AC for up to 10 minutes, requiring concentration to maintain.

Glyph of the Echoing Past: This glyph looks like an abstract image of a human-like figure with waves emanating from it. When activated, it casts the spell Echoing Fear (spell save DC 15). Those who fail a Wisdom saving throw see disturbing images from their past, becoming frightened for 1 minute. They may repeat the saving throw at the end of each of their turns to end the effect on themselves.

Glyph of the Restless Dead: This glyph appears to be a stylized skull. When activated, it casts Speak with Dead on a recently deceased creature within 10 feet, forcing the corpse to answer a single question truthfully, though the answer may be cryptic or vague.

Glyph of the Hidden Path: This glyph looks like a maze with multiple entrances but only one correct exit. When activated, it casts Pass without Trace on all creatures within a 30-foot radius. The glyph's magic gives a +10 bonus to Dexterity (Stealth) checks and can't be tracked except by magical means. It does not leave behind any tracks or other traces of its passage for an hour.

Lair Actions

The Broken Spire and its entrance are imbued with ancient magic, and they react to those who seek to enter without due caution. On initiative count 20 (losing all initiative ties), the entrance to the Broken Spire can take a lair action to cause one of the following effects:

- The Glyph of the Wandering Path activates, casting confusion in a 20-foot radius centered on a point it can see within 60 feet of it (spell save DC 15). The effect requires concentration, which the glyph maintains for 1 minute or until it uses this lair action again.

- Three glyphs in the entrance (chosen randomly) glow brightly. Anyone looking at the glyphs must make a DC 15 Constitution saving throw or be blinded until the end of their next turn.

- The Glyph of the Silent Whisper activates. All creatures within 30 feet of the entrance must succeed on a DC 15 Wisdom saving throw or all sound is silenced in that area until the next round.

These lair actions can't be used two rounds in a row. The glyphs deactivating at the end of a round is a clear indication of this break. The magic of the entrance is clearly old and powerful, but it needs to gather its strength to protect the Spire continuously.

The Crumbling Courtyard

The Crumbling Courtyard is an open area within the Broken Spire that was once a space for magical practice and discussion. Now, it is overgrown and houses a menacing Shatterbeast, a creature born out of the raw energies from the Shattering. This encounter will provide the party with their first combat experience within the Spire, giving them a taste of the dangerous creatures lurking within. It's also an opportunity to discover more about the Shatterbeast and its origins.

As the players step out from the gloom of the entrance hall, they are greeted by an eerie open-air expanse surrounded by high, vine-entangled walls of the Broken Spire. Thorns protrude menacingly from the creeping vines, and shattered statues of what seem to be wizards and scholars lie forgotten, half-hidden by the relentless vegetation. In the middle of the courtyard, there's a sense of foreboding, and the ground seems disturbed, scarred by massive claw marks.

The Shatterbeast is a terrifying creature, a product of magic gone awry during the Shattering. It is ferocious, territorial, and especially aggressive to those who wield magic. This creature should provide a formidable challenge for the party, with high hit points, strong melee attacks, and some resistance to magic.

Also, you may want to consider a peaceful resolution: the Shatterbeast might be reasoned with if approached cautiously and respectfully, especially by a party member with a connection to wild, raw magic.

Lair Actions

At initiative count 20 (losing initiative ties), the Shatterbeast can use a lair action to trigger one of the following effects; it can't use the same effect two rounds in a row:

The Shatterbeast causes the thorny vines in the area to grow rapidly, creating difficult terrain in a 20-foot radius centered on a point it can see within 60 feet of it. The area remains difficult terrain until cleared, which requires at least 1 minute of work.

The Shatterbeast lets out a deafening roar. Each creature of the beast's choice within 120 feet of the beast that can hear the roar must make a DC 15 Wisdom saving throw or become frightened for 1 minute. A creature can repeat the saving throw at the end of each of its turns, ending the effect on itself on a success. If a creature's saving throw is successful or the effect ends for it, the creature is immune to the Shatterbeast's Terrifying Roar for the next 24 hours.

Raw magic from the Shatterbeast oozes through the vines and makes them explode, launching the thorns. The difficult terrain caused by Overgrowth gets cleared in a five-foot radius, centered on a point within 60 feet that the Shatterbeast can see. All creatures in a space that gets cleared, must make a DC 15 Dexterity saving throw. A target takes 4d4 piercing damage on a failed save, or half as much damage on a successful one.

Monster

Shatterbeast

Reward

If the players manage to defeat the Shatterbeast or otherwise pacify it, they find a small hoard that the creature has collected. This treasure includes a collection of shiny trinkets worth about 100 GP, an old silver amulet set with a large sapphire (worth 250 GP), and a Potion of Greater Healing hidden amongst the clutter.

Archmage's Quarters

The private quarters of the Archmage Quillara the Riftweaver, mostly intact but showing signs of a rapid departure. Here, players can find clues about Archmage Quillara's research and maybe personal objects that might hold magical or sentimental value. This encounter is more than just a trap - it is a lore treasure trove and a major plot point. The Characters will gain knowledge about Archmage Quillara and the Rift Shard, along with obtaining or destroying the Nexus Locket based on their alliance.

You step into a room that feels suspended in time, untouched by the chaos of the Shattering. A vast bookshelf filled with arcane tomes and scrolls cover one wall. An ornate desk sits in one corner, scattered with parchment and quills. Opposite the desk, an opulent four-poster bed draped in fine silks lies untouched. Dim light seeps in through a shattered stained-glass window, casting vibrant patterns on the stone floor. The air is heavy with a dormant magic that clings to every artifact in the room.

Characters Aligned to the Iron Conclave

Characters must destroy the Nexus Locket. The Conclave believes that the locket is a source of uncontrolled magic that risks further destabilizing the world. Destroying it will require a powerful spell or a hard strike from a magic weapon.

Characters Aligned to the Underground Resistance

The Resistance sees the Nexus Locket as a beacon of hope, a tool to restore balance. Characters must retrieve it and bring it back to to the camp. However, they must handle it carefully as it is volatile and might unleash a surge of wild magic if mishandled.

Trap: Arcane Glyphs

The Nexus Locket is protected by a complex glyph trap set up by Archmage Quillara. When a character attempts to pick up the Nexus Locket without deactivating the glyphs, it triggers a force explosion. Any creature within a 10-foot radius must make a DC 16 Dexterity saving throw, taking 4d8 force damage on a failed save, or half as much damage on a successful one. Disabling the trap requires successful DC 16 Arcana and Thieves' Tools checks, representing the need to understand and carefully manipulate the arcane glyphs.

Archmage's Notes
Sketches and Diagrams of the Rift Shard

"The Rift Shard continues to astound and terrify me in equal measure. Its structure is unlike anything I have ever seen. Crystalline lattices contain vast, untapped magical potential, akin to a reservoir waiting to be harnessed. However, I must tread carefully - the power within this artifact is potentially cataclysmic."

Writings about the Potential of the Rift Shard to Cause Magical Instability

"My research suggests a terrifying possibility. If misused, the Rift Shard could disrupt the fabric of magic itself, casting our world into a chaos of unpredictable spells and wild surges. This knowledge weighs heavily on my shoulders. The power of creation also holds the potential for untold destruction."

Notes about the Potential of the Rift Shard to Destroy All Magic

"A darker revelation, still. Should the Shard's magic be inverted, it could extinguish the very essence of magic, reducing us to mere mundanity. This concept, a world devoid of enchantment, of arcane knowledge... it chills me to the core. But knowledge is neither good nor evil – it's the application that matters. I must ensure this information does not fall into the wrong hands."

Descriptions of a Theoretical Procedure to Use the Rift Shard to Stabilize Magic

"Perhaps there is hope, however. By carefully aligning the Shard's magical axis with that of our world, I believe we could achieve something remarkable: a stabilization of magic, a perfect equilibrium. The methods to accomplish this are intricate and fraught with danger, but the potential benefits are beyond imagination."

A Journal Entry Expressing Hope for a New Age of Prosperity Through Controlled Magic

"Should I succeed, we could usher in a new era. A world where magic is predictable and safe, where the harmful surges and unpredictable spells are a thing of the past. We could build, heal, create like never before. The potential is boundless. But the path is treacherous, the stakes astronomically high. I can only hope that I am up to the task, for the future of magic, of our world, depends on it."

Locating the Nexus Locket
Finding the Nexus Locket requires a successful DC 16 Investigation check. It is hidden within a secret compartment in Quillara's desk.

Lair Actions
At initiative count 20 (losing initiative ties), the room reacts to its intruders. The room can do the following:

Surge of Arcane Energy: The dormant magic in the room suddenly surges, forcing every creature in the room to make a DC 15 Constitution saving throw or take 2d6 force damage.

Whispers of the Past: Ghostly whispers fill the room, distracting all creatures. Each creature must succeed on a DC 15 Wisdom saving throw or have disadvantage on the next attack roll, ability check, or saving throw it makes before the end of its next turn.

The Lost Library

A once grand library filled with decaying books and scrolls. Some of them might still contain bits of arcane knowledge or historical lore, while others might crumble at the touch.

The Lost Library is a grand testament to the knowledge of ages past. It's a large, dome-like room filled with towering bookshelves. Dusty volumes, ancient scrolls, and decaying manuscripts are crammed into every available space. In the dim light of flickering magical lamps, you can see the faded glory of what was once a center of enlightenment and learning.

Scattered around the room are tables piled high with open books and parchment, ink pots and quills, suggesting someone has been studying here recently. A sour-faced elderly man, hunched over an ancient tome, glares at you from under bushy white eyebrows as you enter - Curator Marvus, the guardian of this library.

The Lost Library encounter is centered around gaining the trust of the eccentric scholar, Curator Marvus. It's a test of wit, knowledge, and diplomatic finesse. The players will need to convince Marvus of their genuine interest in knowledge and their commitment to use it wisely. Remember, Marvus values intellect and respect for his collection above all else.

This is a unique opportunity for players to gain information about the world of the New Dark Age, the Broken Spire, and the secrets they hold. The library is an information goldmine, and Marvus, albeit grumpy and paranoid, can prove to be a valuable ally and source of arcane wisdom.

Characters Aligned to Iron Conclave

Marvus is suspicious of anyone affiliated with the Iron Conclave, given their disregard for knowledge and their destructive methods. However, if the characters can prove their personal commitment to preserving knowledge and their disapproval of the Conclave's methods, they can earn Marvus' trust. They could offer to recover lost books, help Marvus in organizing the library, or promise to use the knowledge they gain against the Conclave's dogmatic approach.

Characters Aligned to Underground Resistance

Marvus is more open to the Underground Resistance, as he considers them less destructive than the Conclave. However, they still need to show their respect for the knowledge and their willingness to use it responsibly. They could promise to spread the knowledge among the Resistance, assisting in educating others, or convince Marvus about the importance of their mission and how the library could aid in stabilizing magic.

Gaining Trust of Curator Marvus

The characters can gain Marvus' trust through various methods. They could:

- Engage him in a discussion on a topic of arcane or historical knowledge. A successful Intelligence (Arcana or History) check could impress Marvus (DC 15 for a respectful discussion, DC 20 to genuinely impress him).
- Show reverence for the books and scrolls, and express their wish to preserve the knowledge contained within them.
- Offer to help him in maintaining the library. This could involve a physical task (such as moving books or cleaning the area, requiring a successful Strength or Dexterity check), or a mental task (such as helping catalog the books, requiring a successful Intelligence check).

If they have any book or piece of unique information, they could offer it to the library's collection.

List of Books in the Library

"Tales of the Pre-Shattering Age" by Alistair the Bard

Description: A compilation of stories, legends, and songs from the time before the Shattering. While some parts are exaggerated or fantastical, the book provides a good understanding of what life was like before magic was destabilized.

DM Notes: This book can provide useful historical context, helping characters understand the drastic changes caused by the Shattering. It could also serve as a source of inspiration or hope, reminding them of what they're fighting for.

"The Theory of Magical Fluctuations" by Magus Corallium

Description: This is a theoretical tome exploring the nature of magical instability and fluctuations. It's a dense read, full of mathematical equations and magical diagrams.

DM Notes: Studying this book could provide a bonus to Arcana checks related to understanding or controlling unstable magic.

"Artifacts of Power: A Compendium" by Sage Dalerion:

Description: A catalogue of powerful artifacts known to the author, along with their descriptions and supposed abilities. The Rift Shard and the Nexus Locket are briefly mentioned, but the details are sketchy at best.

DM Notes: This book might provide clues about other artifacts that could aid the characters in their mission. Use the list of Magic Items later in the book to provide details about each item. This will give the characters insight to which items to look for on their adventure.

"The Fall of the Archmages: A Historical Analysis" by Historian Yorven

Description: A historical analysis of the downfall of the Archmages during the Shattering, exploring their roles, actions, and ultimate fates.

DM Notes: This book could provide vital context about the Archmages and their possible motivations, potentially guiding the characters in their decisions or dealings with remnants of the Archmages' works. Below are notes on the three Archmages that were fundamental to the Shattering occurring:

Archmage Eldrion the Eternity Seeker

Specialization: Eldrion was known for his studies into the essence of time and the nature of immortality.

Historical Analysis: Eldrion was the visionary behind the grand ritual that triggered The Shattering. Driven by an insatiable quest for immortality and timeless knowledge, Eldrion believed that tapping into the raw source of magic would unlock the secrets of eternity. He argued that this would bring about an age of unlimited magical prowess, transcending mortal limitations.

His charisma and influence brought other mages into his ambitious project. However, his obsession blinded him to the risks of tampering with such raw, primal forces. During the ritual, Eldrion was at the heart of the magical storm, directing the energies. When the ritual spun out of control, Eldrion was instantly consumed by the unleashed magic. Some say his spirit still lingers near the Broken Spire, trapped in a temporal loop as a cruel twist of his eternal quest.

Archmage Quillara the Riftweaver

Specialization: Quillara specialized in the magic of dimensions and portals, exploring the unknown territories beyond the mortal realm.

Historical Analysis: Quillara played a key role in the catastrophic ritual by opening a direct gateway to the raw source of magic. She was drawn to Eldrion's plan due to her own curiosity about what lay beyond the mortal plane. Quillara's obsession with exploring the infinite dimensions led her to neglect the potential consequences of her actions on her own world.

Quillara's fate remains a mystery. When The Shattering occurred, she vanished without a trace. Some theories suggest she was thrown into a different dimension, forever lost to the chaos of the multiverse. Other tales whisper of occasional dimensional rifts appearing, thought to be Quillara trying to find her way back.

Archmage Thoren the Arcane Artificer

Specialization: Thoren was a master artificer, renowned for crafting powerful magical artifacts and tools.

Historical Analysis: Thoren was responsible for creating the arcane mechanism designed to harness and contain the raw magical energy, with the Rift Shard as the power for his mechanism. Intrigued by the prospect of creating an artifact of unparalleled power, he threw himself into the project. His overconfidence in his own creations and underestimation of the raw magical energy were his downfall.

Thoren's end came from his own device. As The Shattering unfolded, the artifact meant to contain the energy shattered, releasing a blast of raw magic that incinerated him instantly. His demise serves as a grim reminder of the destructive power of unchecked ambition and overconfidence. His shattered artifact is a symbol of The Shattering, representing the hubris of the Archmages and the devastating consequences of their actions.

"The Nature and Nurture of Magical Creatures" by Beastmaster Thalia

Description: An exhaustive guide to various magical creatures, including their habitats, behaviors, strengths, and weaknesses.

DM Notes: Reading this book could allow characters the ability to make Nature checks related to magical creatures where they normally wouldn't be able to, which could provide non-magic users useful insights when dealing with such creatures in the future. Additionally, they can roll this Nature check at advantage once per long rest.

Lair Actions

On initiative count 20 (losing initiative ties), Curator Marvus can use his intimate knowledge of the library to call upon the arcane energies lingering in the ancient texts. He can use one of the following lair actions:

Arcane Eruption: Marvus selects one book or scroll within the library. It erupts in a burst of magical energy. Each creature within a 10-foot radius must make a DC 15 Dexterity saving throw, taking 3d6 force damage on a failed save, or half as much damage on a successful one.

Summon Lorebound Spirits: Marvus summons the spirits of scholars past, bound to the library. These spirits manifest as spectral figures and attempt to grapple a creature Marvus can see within 30 feet (using Marvus' spellcasting ability modifier for the grapple check). The creature remains grappled until the start of Marvus' next turn or until it breaks free.

Whispers of the Forgotten: Marvus targets one creature he can see within 60 feet. The target must succeed on a DC 15 Wisdom saving throw or begin hearing the whispers of lost knowledge in their mind, becoming stunned until the start of Marvus' next turn.

Marvus can't use the same effect two rounds in a row. The Lost Library is not inherently malicious, but it will protect its keeper and itself if threatened. The lair actions cease if Marvus is incapacitated or leaves the library.

The Hall of Mirrors

The Hall of Mirrors serves as a reflective haunt for the remnants of magical practitioners known as Arcane Echoes. This encounter should emphasize the eerie and disorienting effect of the mirrors, alongside the unpredictable presence of Arcane Echoes. The players must navigate the hall, confront the Echoes, and understand the destructive magic that brought them into being.

The Hall of Mirrors is an unsettling labyrinth of polished, reflective surfaces, creating a seemingly endless expanse of corridors and archways. The light in this area is refracted in strange and disorienting patterns, making it difficult to judge distances or directions. The mirrors, some cracked and others still in perfect condition, depict distorted reflections of the adventurers, often replicating their movements with a slight delay. The air is thick with the faint whispers of the past, and the ethereal Arcane Echoes can be seen drifting slowly through the mirrors, their spectral forms flickering in and out of view.

Characters Aligned to Iron Conclave

For the Iron Conclave, the Hall of Mirrors serves as an eerie classroom where they can unravel the secrets of The Shattering. Characters are encouraged to study the Arcane Echoes, both as a curiosity of arcane aftermath and as a way to better understand the control over the Rift Shard.

The Characters can attempt an Arcana check with a DC of 18 to decipher the spectral remnants' patterns, gaining insights into their formation and the magic that led to their creation. A successful check could reveal that the Arcane Echoes were victims of wild magic surges, potentially providing clues on controlling the Rift Shard's instability.

Additionally, they might try a DC 15 Charisma (Persuasion) check to calm an Arcane Echo long enough to attempt communication. This could involve a delicate series of interactions as they try to assure the Echo of their intentions. Successful communication with an Arcane Echo could reveal further information about the Rift Shard's power, the nature of its magic, or hints about the final moments of The Shattering and clues to how magic can finally be eradicated.

Characters Aligned to Underground Resistance

The Underground Resistance hopes to free these trapped spirits, providing them the peace denied to them in their violent end. It's a mission of mercy, but also a vow to prevent such magic from running rampant again. Characters could try a DC 17 Wisdom (Religion) check to perform a ritual to soothe an Arcane Echo, releasing it from its torment.

Successfully soothing an Echo might reveal glimpses of the Echo's past life, potentially providing insights about the Rift Shard or the past world. Further, by observing the transformation of the Echo upon its release, the Characters might glean information about how to stabilize magic in the Rift Shard. A successful DC 20 Intelligence (Investigation) check might allow a PC to understand the change in the magical energy of the Echo upon release, linking it to the inherent instability of the Rift Shard.

In terms of creature encounters, each of these attempts to communicate or soothe the Echoes will inevitably draw the attention of other Echoes in the Hall, potentially leading to combat encounters. Utilize Arcane Echoes as presented above for such encounters. Allow for creative uses of the Hall's mirrors during these encounters, possibly allowing for unique battle strategies.

Responses from an Arcane Echo

Response 1: "I felt the weave unravel...it wasn't meant to happen...the Shard..."

DM Note: This confirms the Rift Shard's involvement in The Shattering.

For the **Iron Conclave**, this information solidifies their belief in the Shard's destructive power and its potential use as a weapon.

For the **Underground Resistance**, this highlights the danger of the Rift Shard and the urgency to stabilize it.

Response 2: "The Archmage... she was desperate...the spell went awry..."

DM Note: This implicates the Archmage and a spell gone wrong.

For the **Iron Conclave**, this suggests the possibility that control over the Shard might be achieved through understanding the Archmage's spellwork.

For the **Underground Resistance**, this could motivate them to find more of the Archmage's notes or research to prevent a repeat of this tragedy.

Response 3: "We wanted prosperity...new era of magic...but the cost...so high..."

DM Note: This indicates that The Shattering was an unintended consequence of a spell intended to bring about a new magical age.

For the **Iron Conclave**, this is evidence that the Archmage's ambition wasn't innately malicious. With greater control, they could harness the Rift Shard's power without repeating his mistake.

For the **Underground Resistance**, this speaks to the danger of unchecked power and the importance of balance. They might be inspired to find a way to harness the Shard's power for restoration, rather than destruction.

Response 4: "Unstable...too much...need a...stabilizer..."

DM Note: This suggests the need for a stabilizer to control the Rift Shard's power.

For the **Iron Conclave**, this could mean seeking a magical item or conducting a ritual to stabilize the Shard and harness its power.

For the **Underground Resistance**, this reinforces the idea that the Shard's power can be controlled and used for good. They might seek the Nexus Locket or a similar magical device to stabilize the Shard.

Response 5: "Free us...end the cycle...balance must be restored..."

DM Note: This echoes a plea for peace and the restoration of balance.

For the **Iron Conclave**, this might serve as a sobering reminder of the cost of their ambition.

For the **Underground Resistance**, this will likely resonate deeply with their goals, reinforcing the necessity of their mission to restore balance and prevent further harm.

Lair Actions

On initiative count 20 (losing initiative ties), the Arcane Echo can manipulate the reflective surfaces in the Hall of Mirrors, causing the following effects:

Mirror Illusions: The Arcane Echo can cause one mirror to show misleading images. Any creature within sight of the mirror must make a DC 15 Wisdom saving throw or become confused, as per the confusion spell, until the start of the Arcane Echo's next turn.

Reflective Barrier: The Arcane Echo bends the light around itself, creating a shield of refracted energy. Until the start of its next turn, all attack rolls against it have disadvantage.

Mirror Step: The Arcane Echo enters a mirror within its sight and reappears from another mirror within 60 feet.

The Arcane Echo can't use the same effect two rounds in a row. The lair actions cease if the Arcane Echo is incapacitated or leaves the hall.

Monster

Arcane Echo

The Warped Laboratory

An area of the Spire where wild magic is most potent. It's a maze of twisted walls and distorted reality, remnants of magical experiments gone awry.

The bizarre room stretches before you, an eerie tableau of chaos and wonder. The walls, floor, and ceiling shimmer with an almost luminescent quality, distorted by the rampant magic that has touched every corner of this place. It's as if reality itself has become pliable, bent and twisted into unfamiliar forms that are at once fascinating and unsettling.

Crystals of myriad hues grow like bizarre stalactites from the ceiling and sprout from the floor like a carpet of jagged, gleaming spikes. Each crystal pulses with a light of its own, lending the space a strangely beautiful, shifting glow. A closer look reveals that these are not ordinary crystals but petrified spell residues, capturing within them the echo of magic that once shaped and governed this realm.

Here and there, rifts in the very fabric of reality gape open like hungry maws. They flicker and waver, their edges shimmering like a heat mirage. Through these rifts, you catch glimpses of the Ethereal Plane, a shadowy reflection of your own reality.

Strange devices, the remnants of powerful magical experiments, are strewn across the area. Among these, a machine that throbs with a palpable force stands out.

This is a place where the rules of nature are rewritten, where imagination has been given free rein. Yet it's also a place of danger, its unpredictable energy capable of awe-inspiring creation just as much as it is of catastrophic destruction. To navigate this landscape is to dance on the razor's edge between order and chaos, knowledge and oblivion. It's a haunting reminder of the catastrophic event that brought about the New Dark Age, and a testament to the unfathomable power and potential of magic itself.

The Warped Laboratory is a testament to the horrifying power of The Shattering. It's a disorienting, dangerous place that serves as the living quarters for The Shattered, beings whose bodies and minds were irrevocably warped by the event. Characters should approach with caution and empathy. The encounter's difficulty can be modified by adjusting the number of The Shattered present and the intensity of the environmental hazards. This encounter is ideal for showcasing the physical and psychological toll of The Shattered, as well as the far-reaching consequences of uncontrolled magic.

Characters Aligned to Iron Conclave

The Iron Conclave sees The Warped Laboratory as a stark reminder of the destructive potential of magic. They wish to study the effects of wild magic here in order to better understand how to combat it and ultimately eliminate it. A DC 15 Arcana check allows them to identify key elements of the warped magic, providing insight into potential weaknesses of magical creatures or effects (DM's discretion for the exact effects, but possibilities include granting advantage on the next saving throw against a magical effect, or understanding a magical creature's vulnerability, etc.). Their goal in this encounter is not to harness magic, but rather to unravel it, find its weak points and, if possible, permanently neutralize the chaos.

Characters Aligned to Underground Resistance

For the Underground Resistance, the Warped Laboratory is a poignant testament to the disastrous consequences of uncontrolled magic. Seeing the warped reality, they are further motivated to prevent any further magic-induced catastrophes.

Their first objective might be to try and rectify the warped reality, hoping to find a way to stabilize the area. This could involve trying to understand and neutralize the Warp Field Generator. They could attempt an Arcana check of DC 20 to figure out how to disable or reverse the generator, thus calming the chaotic magic in the surrounding area.

The Ethereal Rift could serve as a crucial point of interest for the Resistance. With a successful Arcana check of DC 20, they might be able to stabilize the rift, allowing for brief periods of passage to the Ethereal Plane. This could aid them in understanding the complex connections between different planes, potentially revealing ways to combat magic catastrophes in the future.

Next, the spell residue crystals could offer valuable insights into the past, before the Shattering. These crystals hold trapped spells, and with a DC 15 Arcana check, Resistance members might be able to release and decipher these spells, giving them knowledge of past magic and potentially how to counteract the effects of such magic.

Finally, the Unstable Magical Cores and the Matter Transmutation Unit offer tantalizing prospects of utilizing the wild magic for the resistance's benefit. A successful interaction (Arcana DC 15) with the cores could grant a temporary boost in their magical defenses or abilities, while safely dismantling and studying the transmutation unit (Arcana DC 20) could provide them with crucial information about magical transformation processes and how to control or prevent them.

Experiments in the Warped Laboratory

Spell Residue Crystallization: Shimmering crystals with captured spells inside them. Interacting (Arcana DC 15) can release the spell residue, providing invaluable insight into the mechanics of spellcasting.

Iron Conclave: The Conclave might use this insight to understand the underlying principles of magic, leading them closer to its eradication.

Underground Resistance: Resistance members could use these spells to aid in their efforts, expanding their knowledge and arsenal of magic.

Ethereal Rift: A tear in the fabric of reality that leads to the Ethereal Plane. A successful DC 20 Arcana check can stabilize it for short-term use.

Iron Conclave: The Conclave can study this rift to understand the potential consequences and risks of unrestrained magic, strengthening their resolve to annihilate it.

Underground Resistance: Resistance members could use this as an escape route or a place to hide or rest.

Warp Field Generator: A device that generates a field of wild magic. Disabling it (Arcana DC 20) might calm the surrounding area, making The Shattered less aggressive.

Iron Conclave: The Conclave might want to dismantle the generator to learn more about how to prevent such devices from existing in the future, moving one step closer to a world without magic.

Underground Resistance: Resistance members might want to disable it to make the area safer for themselves and The Shattered.

Unstable Magical Cores: Energy cores containing wild magic. Interacting (Arcana DC 15) can drain some energy, granting an understanding of the volatile and dangerous nature of wild magic.

Iron Conclave: The Conclave could study these cores to learn about the instability of magic and find ways to neutralize it.

Underground Resistance: Resistance members could use the energy to increase their chances of success in their mission.

Arcane Mutation Chamber: A containment field that has a low chance to transform mundane objects or creatures into magical entities when exposed for a prolonged period (Arcana DC 20 to understand the process).

Iron Conclave: Members of the Conclave may wish to study this transformation to understand how magic corrupts and changes the natural order, reinforcing their conviction to eradicate it.

Underground Resistance: Resistance members might cautiously use the chamber to imbue mundane objects with magical properties, offering potential advantages in their resistance efforts.

Reality Warp Gauge: A peculiar device that measures the intensity of magical distortions in reality. Properly reading the gauge (Arcana DC 15) can offer insights into fluctuations of magical energies in the vicinity.

Iron Conclave: The Conclave might use this information to identify areas of high magic concentration for their containment and eradication efforts.

Underground Resistance: Resistance members could use the gauge to avoid areas of high magic concentration, to safeguard themselves and prevent exacerbation of the effects of magic.

Lair Actions

On initiative count 20 (losing initiative ties), the erratic energy surging through the Warped Laboratory destabilizes, triggering one of the following effects. Roll a d6 to determine which effect takes place.

Gravity Distortion: The force of gravity suddenly reverses in a 20-foot-radius sphere centered on a point the DM chooses within the Laboratory. Creatures in the area must succeed on a DC 15 Strength saving throw or be lifted from the ground, becoming restrained and taking 1d6 force damage as they crash into the ceiling. This effect ends at the start of the next lair action, dropping affected creatures and potentially causing fall damage.

Time Dilation: Time within a 20-foot-radius sphere centered on a point the DM chooses within the Laboratory fluctuates wildly. Each creature in the area must make a DC 15 Constitution saving throw. On a failed save, the creature is aged by 1d10 years. On a successful save, the creature becomes younger by 1d10 years. Age changes last until dispelled or until the creature leaves the Laboratory.

Spatial Rupture: A tear in space appears at a point the DM chooses within the Laboratory, remaining open until the start of the next lair action. Any creature that starts its turn within 10 feet of the spatial rupture must succeed on a DC 15 Dexterity saving throw or be pulled 1d10 feet toward it.

Arcane Surge: Wild magic energy explodes in a 20-foot-radius sphere centered on a point the DM chooses within the Laboratory. Each creature in the area must succeed on a DC 15 Constitution saving throw or take 2d10 force damage and be stunned until the end of their next turn.

Reality Warp: The surroundings within a 20-foot-radius sphere centered on a point the DM chooses within the Laboratory morph and twist. The area becomes difficult terrain, and any creature that starts its turn in the area must succeed on a DC 15 Wisdom saving throw or be incapacitated by the mind-bending transformation of reality until the start of its next turn.

Elemental Chaos: The magic of the Laboratory generates a spontaneous manifestation of one of the four elements in a 20-foot-radius sphere centered on a point the DM chooses within the Laboratory. Roll a d4 to determine the manifested element: 1 - Fire, 2 - Ice, 3 - Lightning, 4 – Earth (bludgeoning). Each creature in the area must make a DC 15 Dexterity saving throw, taking 2d10 damage of the appropriate type on a failed save, or half as much damage on a successful one.

These effects add to the unpredictable, chaotic nature of the Warped Laboratory and should reinforce to the players the inherent dangers and unpredictability of this location.

The Echo Chamber

A room that magnifies sound and potentially energy. Any spell cast here might have unpredictable effects. The room also has a group of captured **Resistance** members that the Iron Conclave have been holding prisoner.

The Echo Chamber is a vast circular room with towering walls that curve into a domed ceiling. The room is eerily silent until you step inside, where even the softest whisper echoes and amplifies into a resounding sound. The walls are adorned with a variety of complex arcane symbols that pulse gently with magical energy, giving the room a faint, multi-colored glow. A group of captives - members of the Underground Resistance - huddle together at the center of the room. Around them, the floor is inscribed with a radiant glyph, glowing with latent power.

The Echo Chamber offers a unique encounter that tests the Characters' resourcefulness and restraint. Casting spells in the Echo Chamber can have amplified and unpredictable effects due to the unique magical resonance of the room. This can be used as a tool or a deterrent, depending on the situation. Captured Resistance members provide a clear objective, and the Iron Conclave presence gives an opposition. However, the challenge is further complicated by a trap encircling the captives. Consider your party's abilities and tendencies when preparing this encounter to ensure a challenging but feasible scenario.

Characters Aligned to Iron Conclave

Iron Conclave members recognize the Echo Chamber's potential for their ultimate goal of eradicating magic. By experimenting with the resonance effects of the room, they hope to discover a way to counteract or negate magical energy. The Conclave will try to protect this room and its captives who serve as test subjects. With a successful Arcana check (DC 15), Conclave members can attempt to manipulate the room's amplification effect, potentially disrupting magic-casting attempts or creating false sensory inputs. Knowledge on how the effect works can then be created into weapons that can be used in battles.

Characters Aligned to Underground Resistance

The Resistance aims to free their comrades and escape without triggering the room's protective glyph. They may also wish to understand the Echo Chamber's unique properties to find a way to counteract the Iron Conclave's plans. A successful Investigation check (DC 15) can reveal the nature of the glyph, while a successful Dexterity check (using Thieves' Tools) DC 15 or Dispel Magic can disable it. Characters can instead choose to make an Arcana check (DC 15) to identify the nature of the glyph trap, and a second one (DC 18) to attempt to disable it. Characters will still need to disable the Echo Trap in addition to the glyph.

The Echo Trap

The trap in the Echo Chamber is not a conventional one. Instead of relying on hidden mechanisms or magical glyphs, this trap uses the room's unique acoustics to amplify sound to potentially lethal levels. Any sound made within the room will steadily grow louder and more intense, causing physical harm and disorientation.

The trap activates as soon as a sound is made, regardless of its initial volume. However, the volume of the initial sound affects how quickly the echo trap escalates. The amplification is divided into five levels:

Level 1 - Soft Sounds (whispering, light footfalls): Initial amplification is slow, taking about 1 minute to reach harmful levels. A DC 10 Constitution saving throw is needed every minute to avoid taking 1d4 thunder damage and being deafened for 1 round.

Level 2 - Normal Conversation (talking, rustling items): Amplification is quicker, taking about 30 seconds to reach harmful levels. A DC 15 Constitution saving throw is needed every 30 seconds to avoid taking 2d4 thunder damage and being deafened for 2 rounds.

Level 3 - Loud Noises (yelling, combat noises): Amplification is nearly instant, taking about 10 seconds to reach harmful levels. A DC 20 Constitution saving throw is needed every 10 seconds to avoid taking 3d4 thunder damage and being deafened for 3 rounds.

Level 4 - Very Loud Noises (thunderous spells, shattering glass): Amplification is instant, causing immediate harm. A DC 25 Constitution saving throw is needed immediately to avoid taking 4d4 thunder damage and being deafened for 4 rounds.

Level 5 - Deafening Sounds (explosions, dragon roars): The immediate echo is devastating. A DC 30 Constitution saving throw is needed immediately to avoid taking 5d4 thunder damage and being deafened for 5 rounds.

Disabling the Trap

The echo trap can't be disarmed in the traditional sense since it's an intrinsic part of the room's acoustics. However, there are a few potential ways to manage it:

Silence: Casting the Silence spell can nullify the echo trap. Characters will not be able to speak but will be able to communicate safely with written notes or hand gestures within its radius. However, any sound made outside the Silence spell's area will still trigger the echo trap.

Softly Treading: Moving quietly and communicating non-verbally (e.g., using sign language or written notes) can keep the echo trap at Level 1, minimizing its potential harm.

Disruptive Noise: A constant low-level noise, such as the hum of a Thaumaturgy cantrip or a low drone from a musical instrument, might be able to disrupt the amplification process, acting as a kind of 'white noise' to prevent louder sounds from escalating. This will require an Arcana check (DC 20) to tune the disrupting noise correctly.

Captured Resistance Members

Aria Lightfoot: A former bard whose songs of hope and rebellion have made her a symbol for the Resistance. She's been muted by a cruel spell, but her resolve remains strong.

Thoren Ironhand: A skilled blacksmith who used to fashion magical weapons for the Resistance. He's gruff and serious, but fiercely loyal to his comrades.

Liana Greenwhisper: A druid who communed with the spirits of the land before the Shattering. She's soft-spoken and kind, caring deeply for all forms of life.

Jace Shadowstep: A rogue who used his skills to spy on the Conclave. He's cunning and resourceful, always looking for an escape route.

Elira Starsong: A wizard who studied ancient magic and hopes to stabilize the world's magic. She's intelligent and idealistic, believing in the Resistance's cause with all her heart.

Lair Actions

On initiative count 20 (losing initiative ties), the Echo Chamber amplifies the magical energy in the room, causing a random magical effect to happen. Roll a d10 to determine the effect: 1-2, an echoed spell repeats its effect at its original location; 3-4, an audio wave pushes everyone 10 feet away from the center knocking them off their feet and leaving them prone on the floor for 2 rounds; 5-6, a loud, disorienting sound causes all creatures to be deafened until the start of the next round; 7-8, all lights and sounds within the room are dampened, causing the area to be lightly obscured; 9-10, a surge of healing energy restores 1d8 hit points to all creatures within the room.

The Broken Spire

The broken spire is at the center of the building. Once the residence of Archmage Eldrion the Eternity Seeker, since the Shattering the area has become a haunted location with the Ghost of the Broken Spire, Archmage Quillara the Riftweaver, taking residence.

The Broken Spire rises ominously from the heart of the compound, a towering monument to past splendor and current ruin. Its once proud, stalwart figure is now a skeletal silhouette against the cloudy grey sky. Its grandeur reduced to jagged shards of stone and spectral echoes of a time forgotten.

Rain seeps from the heavens through the Spire's shattered roof, the drops whispering tales of a bygone era as they patter against the fractured stone floor, pooling in the hollows of age-old footprints. The air within the tower is heavy, almost tangible, saturated with the scent of damp earth and ancient stone. This melancholy melody of the rain plays a symphony of the past, each note echoing through the hollowed chambers with an ethereal cadence.

The Spire's walls are marked with the vestiges of former window openings. These empty eyelets gaze out onto the wild, untamed forest that creeps up to the Spire's base, and beyond to the sprawling, rugged countryside. Within these windows, the world outside continues its timeless dance, oblivious to the tragedy that once unfolded within the Spire.

Amid the chaotic wreckage floats the Ghost of the Broken Spire. Draped in the tattered remnants of regal robes, the spectral figure emanates an aura of solemn despair. Her haunting eyes reflect centuries of sorrow and regret, and a resolve forged in the crucible of loss.

The Broken Spire encounter is steeped in history and mystery, revealing the tragic past of the New Dark Age. The Ghost of the Broken Spire, the spectral Archmage Quillara the Riftweaver, is the focal point of this encounter. Depending on the approach of the Characters, she can be a powerful ally, a fount of knowledge, or a hostile opponent. The presence of the Riftblade offers both factions a potential tool in their ongoing struggle.

Characters Aligned to Iron Conclave

The Iron Conclave would want to confront the Ghost of the Broken Spire and learn from her mistakes. They believe that her knowledge could help them find a way to destroy all magic, preventing another catastrophe like The Shattering. The Conclave might also be interested in the Riftblade. While they generally seek to eradicate magic, this weapon could serve as a useful tool in their mission. To find the Riftblade, a PC must succeed on a DC 20 Investigation check while searching the room. The Riftblade will be located hidden in a secured chest. The chest is hidden under a pile of moldy rugs.

Characters Aligned to Underground Resistance

The Underground Resistance sees the Ghost of the Broken Spire as a tragic figure, a reminder of the cost of The Shattering. They would seek to comfort her, learn from her knowledge, and possibly persuade her to aid their cause. They would be very interested in finding the Riftblade, a powerful magical artifact that could help them stabilize magic and restore it to the world. To locate the Riftblade, a PC must succeed on a DC 15 Investigation check while searching the room. The lower DC reflects the Resistance's greater familiarity and affinity with magic and magical artifacts.

Interacting with The Ghost of the Broken Spire

Characters can interact with the Ghost of the Broken Spire through conversation, trying to glean information, persuade her to their cause, or soothe her lingering sorrow. This could involve Wisdom (Insight), Intelligence (History), or Charisma (Persuasion) checks, with the DC depending on the nature of their approach and the information or assistance they're seeking. In addition, you can use the following table and roll a 1d10 to create a random response:

1d10	Type of Response	Words for the Response	DM Notes

#		Quote	Behavior
1	Neutral	"I am but a shadow of a world long gone. Tread carefully among these ruins."	The Ghost remains passive, observing the Characters but not interacting unless directly addressed.
2	Hostile	"You dare intrude upon my solitude? Face the wrath of the Broken Spire!"	The Ghost becomes hostile, potentially attacking the Characters or using her spectral abilities to hinder their progress.
3	Helpful	"Your hearts seem pure, unlike many who have come before. I can offer you some guidance."	The Ghost is willing to share her knowledge and insights about the Spire, The Shattering, or other relevant topics.
4	Despairing	"I am the cause of The Shattering, the harbinger of this age of despair. Leave me to my eternal remorse."	Overwhelmed by her despair, the Ghost fades from view, disappearing for a time. She may reappear later, depending on the Characters' actions.
5	Redemptive	"Perhaps through you, I may find some semblance of redemption. Ask, and I will assist as I am able."	The Ghost is cooperative and willing to aid the Characters, offering her spectral abilities or knowledge to support their cause.
6	Mournful	"Can you hear it? The echoing silence where once laughter and knowledge danced in the air..."	The Ghost retreats into her sorrow, ignoring the Characters as she mourns the loss of the past.
7	Warning	"Beware, intruders. The shadows of this place hold more than just sorrow..."	The Ghost warns the Characters of other potential dangers within the Spire, possibly hinting at traps, hostile entities, or other threats.
8	Pleading	"If you hold any respect for the past, leave this place undisturbed. Do not repeat my mistakes."	The Ghost pleads with the Characters to tread carefully and respect the Spire's past, potentially leading to a decrease in hostility.
9	Confused	"Why do you disturb me? Can you not see the weight of my sorrow?"	The Ghost doesn't understand the Characters' intentions and may react unpredictably to their actions.
10	Defiant	"Though I am but a ghost, I will defend what remains of my home!"	The Ghost rises to defend the Spire, ready to use her spectral abilities to deter or repel intruders.

As the DM, adjust these responses and the subsequent actions of the Ghost based on the Characters' interactions and the evolving narrative of The New Dark Age.

Lair Actions

On initiative count 20 (losing initiative ties), the Ghost of the Broken Spire can cause one of the following magical effects:

Phantom Arcane: The Ghost can draw on the arcane energies still echoing within the Broken Spire. Up to three spells previously cast within the Spire are mimicked by ghostly apparitions. These are mere illusions and do not have the effects of the real spells, but they appear very real and might distract or frighten enemies. Any creature in the room must succeed on a DC 15 Wisdom saving throw or be Frightened until the end of their next turn.

Shattering Tremors: The Ghost can cause a minor tremor as the Spire itself seems to relive the moment of its destruction. Each creature standing on the ground in the room must succeed on a DC 15 Dexterity saving throw or be knocked prone.

Whispers of the Archmage: The Ghost channels her past knowledge and experiences, imbuing one PC with a fleeting piece of arcane wisdom. One PC of the Ghost's choice gains advantage on their next Arcana check.

The Ghost can't use the same effect two rounds in a row. She uses these actions to defend the Spire and deter intruders, or to aid those she deems worthy. As the DM, you can choose the most appropriate action based on the current situation and the Ghost's disposition towards the party.

NPC

Ghost of the Broken Spire

The Undercity

The Undercity

The Undercity is a complex, multi-layered setting that combines elements of mystery, danger, and adventure. It's a place where secrets lie around every corner, and unexpected encounters can occur at any moment. Here are some key points to consider when introducing the Undercity to your players:

Rich History: The Undercity is steeped in ancient lore. It was built by a civilization long forgotten, and its original purpose may still be a mystery. It has been used over the centuries for many purposes – as a burial ground, as a refuge during times of war, as a secret meeting place, and more recently, as a haven for the Underground Resistance. Feel free to drop hints about its history to make your players curious about its past.

Complex Layout: The Undercity is a vast network of tunnels and chambers, all interconnected in a maze-like configuration. Navigating through the Undercity can be a challenge. It's easy to get lost, and unexpected dangers lurk around every corner. Make use of this to create tension and suspense.

Varied Encounters: The Undercity is home to many different creatures, from harmless critters to dangerous monsters. Additionally, traps left by the original builders or recent inhabitants can surprise unwary adventurers. Remember, the Underground Resistance has also set up traps to deter the Iron Conclave patrols.

Factional Activity: Both the Iron Conclave and the Underground Resistance are active in the Undercity. The Iron Conclave patrols regularly, searching for magic users and signs of the Resistance. On the other hand, the Resistance uses the Undercity as a base, a safe haven, and a conduit for moving goods and personnel. Their presence can create additional layers of conflict and intrigue.

Multiple Points of Interest: There are many locations within the Undercity that can serve as points of interest. The Iron Gate, the Crystal Caverns, the Undercity Market, and the Whispering Halls each carry their unique character and story potential. These locales can be the stages for encounters, plot hooks, and challenges.

Dynamic Environment: The environment in the Undercity can be a tool for creating tension and promoting creative problem-solving. Collapsing tunnels, sudden floods, areas of magical instability, and more can add an extra layer of excitement to the exploration.

Travel Time: It is one day walking from the Broken Spire to the Undercity. The Iron Conclave Fortress can be accessed through the Iron Gate.

Remember, the Undercity is a living, breathing environment. Its inhabitants have their own goals and motivations, and their actions can shape the narrative in unexpected ways. Keep the atmosphere tense and the stakes high, and your players will be engrossed in the challenges and mysteries of the Undercity.

As your eyes adjust to the dim, flickering torchlight, you begin to perceive the imposing scale of the Undercity. Stone archways rise up, creating a roof of shadowy stalactites against a ceiling lost in darkness. The way before you fractures into a labyrinth of branching tunnels, each pathway offering its own unseen mysteries and perils.

The air in this subterranean expanse carries a damp, earthy scent, subtly tinged with an undercurrent of arcane energy. The atmosphere reverberates with echoes of dripping water, the scurrying of hidden creatures, and whispers that could be the remnants of ancient magic.

On your left, the cave walls are embedded with radiant crystal formations. These crystals softly pulse with an inner light, scattering a prismatic spray of colors that illuminates the surrounding cavern. The soft glow from within these formations creates an ethereal landscape, its spectral beauty belying its potential dangers.

Further ahead, the remains of a once-grand statue preside over a wide underground plaza. The worn cobblestones beneath your feet are etched with cryptic markings, their meanings eroded by the passage of time.

Through a narrow tunnel to your right, you can see the faint, eerie light of the Iron Gate. Its massive silhouette stands as a harsh contrast to the natural surroundings, its austere form serving as a foreboding entrance to the vast labyrinth beyond.

In the distance, faint murmurs of activity reverberate, hinting at bustling markets and shadowy figures trading arcane wares. Deeper still, the gentle echo of flowing water indicates the presence of underground wells or streams, their rhythmic sound a soothing constant in the labyrinthine Undercity. Welcome, adventurers, to the Undercity, a place of ancient secrets and forgotten lore. As you navigate its winding paths and hidden chambers, remember: while it may offer sanctuary to some, it can also be a perilous maze of darkness and danger. Stay vigilant, keep your blades sharp, and your spells prepared.

The characters can explore the Undercity and find more information on the Rift Shard. The characters can also continue their alignment to either the Iron Conclave or the Underground Resistance. Additional tasks for the Iron Conclave will be presented to the characters if they visit The Iron Gate, and tasks for the Underground Resistance will be given to characters at The Whispering Hall. For your reference, the additional tasks are:

Characters Aligned to Iron Conclave

Cryptic Infiltration: The Iron Conclave has received intelligence about a gathering of magic users within the depths of the Undercity. The players are tasked to infiltrate this gathering, capture or eliminate the magic users, and confiscate any magical items they may possess.

Trap Neutralization: The Resistance has filled the Undercity with numerous magical traps. The Iron Conclave assigns the players to disable these traps to make the Undercity safer for their patrols and to demonstrate the danger posed by unrestrained magic.

Strategic Mapping: The Undercity's tunnels are a convoluted labyrinth. The Iron Conclave needs a detailed map of the network to help them more effectively search for magic users. The party is tasked with exploring the Undercity and creating an accurate map.

Characters Aligned to Underground Resistance

Safe Passage: The Resistance needs to move a group of magic users through the Undercity to safety. The party is entrusted to escort them, ensuring they pass unharmed through the maze of tunnels and past any Iron Conclave patrols.

Magical Cache Recovery: A hidden cache of magical items has been stashed in the Undercity, but its location has been lost. The party is asked to find and retrieve these items before the Iron Conclave does.

Subterranean Sabotage: The Resistance has learned of an impending Iron Conclave raid on the Undercity. The party is tasked with setting up traps and ambushes to slow down or halt the Iron Conclave's advance.

The characters can move on to the final location, the Iron Conclave Fortress, when they have either completed the tasks or they have enough information on how to control the Rift Shard.

The Undercity Entrance

Damp, large pipes lead from above ground to the Undercity where the Underground Resistance and allies of magic are hiding.

The Undercity Entrance is a network of ancient, moss-covered sewer tunnels, now serving as the gateways to the Undercity. The walls of these tunnels are slick with damp and faintly glowing lichen, the air heavy with the musty scent of earth and the echoing drip-drip-drip of water. Echoes of distant magical energies crackle in the air, casting an eerie, flickering light in the otherwise dim tunnels. Sturdy iron gates once barred these entrances, but time and corrosion have left them broken and hanging askew. As the characters delve deeper, the tunnels widen into cavernous chambers, revealing a sprawling labyrinth of stone and magic that is the Undercity.

The Undercity Entrance is an excellent introductory encounter to the Undercity campaign setting. Here, the characters can see firsthand the stark contrast between the city above and the magical underbelly beneath. It's a journey from the known to the unknown, stepping away from the mundane world and into a place where magic pulses through the very stones. This encounter is designed to set the tone for the rest of the adventure, emphasizing the sense of entering an alien world that exists beneath the bustling city streets. It's also a good spot for an initial conflict or encounter to raise the stakes and introduce the factional tensions in the Undercity.

Conclave's Surprise Inspection

The Iron Conclave, suspicious of increased activity near this entrance to the Undercity, has sent a small inspection team to investigate. This team consists of a Conclave Elite Guard, two Conclave Brute Guards, and a Prohibition Construct - a hulking, intimidating construct designed to seek out and neutralize magic.

This encounter could begin with the party noticing the approach of the Conclave's team, giving them a short window of time to hide any magical items or effects, prepare an ambush, or even try to bluff their way through the inspection.

The Prohibition Construct can sense magic within a 30ft radius, and will alert the guards to any magical items or effects it detects. If a fight breaks out, the Conclave guards and the construct will attempt to subdue and capture the party, but they will retreat and call for reinforcements if overwhelmed.

This encounter can provide both combat and social interaction challenges, and it may result in the party learning more about the Conclave's operations and capabilities, depending on how they handle the situation.

DM Note: If the party has been open about their allegiance to the Underground Resistance, you might choose to make this encounter more of a direct confrontation. The Conclave could be attempting to set a trap, or they might send a stronger force to try and capture or eliminate the party. Alternatively, if the party has been working undercover, this could be a tense moment where they have to maintain their cover under close scrutiny.

It's also worth considering how the results of this encounter could affect future events. If the party manages to capture or disable one of the Conclave's Prohibition Constructs, for example, this could provide them with a valuable resource in their struggle against the Conclave. On the other hand, if the party's presence in the area is discovered, this could lead to increased Conclave activity, making future tasks more challenging.

Characters Aligned to Iron Conclave

The Iron Conclave would see these tunnels sealed, cutting off access to the Undercity and trapping the magic users below. They might task the characters with scouting the tunnels for weak points to be collapsed or for tracking the movements of those who enter and leave the Undercity through these entrances. The Conclave might also set ambushes here, aiming to catch Resistance members or magic users unawares as they surface.

Characters Aligned to Underground Resistance

The Resistance needs these tunnels to stay open for their continued operations and the welfare of the magic users in the Undercity. They might ask the characters to protect these entrances against the Iron Conclave, create diversions to misdirect the Conclave patrols, or help smuggle magical individuals or contraband through these tunnels. Maintenance is also crucial, as the tunnels are old and prone to collapse, so the Resistance might need help from skilled artisans or engineers.

Lair Actions

As the entrance to the Undercity, the tunnels are imbued with the lingering magical energies of the Undercity. As a lair action, the DM can have these latent energies react to intruders. On initiative count 20 (losing initiative ties), the lair can take one lair action to cause one of the following magical effects; the lair can't use the same effect two rounds in a row:

The tunnel walls glow brighter, shedding bright light in a 60-foot radius. Any creatures within this area must make a DC 15 Constitution saving throw or be blinded until the end of their next turn.

A sudden gust of wind blows through the tunnels. All creatures must succeed on a DC 15 Strength saving throw or be pushed 10 feet away and knocked prone.

The air becomes heavy and oppressive, sapping the strength of the invaders. Each creature in the lair must succeed on a DC 15 Constitution saving throw or have their speed halved until the end of their next turn.

The magical energies are not under the control of any one individual, so they can potentially harm allies as well as enemies. However, regular dwellers of the Undercity are more accustomed to these sudden magical surges and may have learned ways to protect themselves or avoid the worst of the effects.

Monsters

Conclave Elite Guard, two Conclave Brute Guards, and a Prohibition Construct

The Shadowed Alcoves

This section of the Undercity is a large hall lined with multiple alcoves. Each alcove is large enough to hold a small group, and due to the low lighting, it is hard to see who is inside each one, making it a popular location for secret meetings.

You enter into a large, spacious hall, the ceiling lost in shadow, while a series of soft, low-lit lanterns cast a dim glow across the area. Lining the walls are a multitude of alcoves, each shrouded in a mix of shadow and faint light. The murmurs of hushed conversations echo in the air, and as your eyes adjust, you can make out the shapes of individuals and small groups gathered within these sheltered recesses. It's a sanctuary of whispered secrets and covert meetings.

Characters Aligned to Iron Conclave

The characters will need to infiltrate the Shadowed Alcoves without raising suspicion. Once inside, they should try to disrupt the gathering, which could involve creating a distraction or sparking a panic. For this task, a successful DC 15 Deception or Performance check is required. This area would be a prime target for the **"Trap Neutralization"** task.

Characters Aligned to Underground Resistance

The characters will be tasked with monitoring the entrance to the alcoves, requiring a Perception check with a DC of an intruder's Stealth check, if applicable, to notice any suspicious activity. If an intrusion is detected, they must swiftly protect the magic users present at the meeting, which could lead to combat encounters. Use the Random Encounter table later in the book to create a random intrusion.

Alcoves

There are four alcoves where characters and NPCs can meet. Each alcove is protected by a trap. These traps serve a dual purpose for the Underground Resistance: they provide a layer of protection for the magic users meeting in the alcoves, and they also function as a test, sifting out allies of the Resistance from those who would harm them. It's a testament to the creative ways the Underground Resistance uses magic for their cause.

Alcove 1

Occupants: Sorceress Elandra and Elowen the Green.

Conversation: Elandra and Elowen are engrossed in conversation. Elandra discusses the properties of the Shard, explaining how it could potentially stabilize the disruptive energies of the Shattering. Elowen listens attentively, nodding, as she ponders how this stabilization could restore the natural order, providing a way to harmonize magic and nature once again. Their conversation holds a sense of desperate hope; they believe in the potential the Rift Shard holds for restoring the magical balance.

Trap Name: The Aura of Silence

Description: This trap, guarding the first alcove, is an enchantment that envelops the alcove in a sphere of silence. The Aura of Silence trap is triggered by proximity. When a creature moves within 10 feet of the alcove, the enchantment activates, enveloping the alcove in a sphere of silence.

Effect if Triggered: Any sound within or passing through a 20-foot-radius sphere centered on the alcove is silenced. No noise can be created within or pass through the sphere. Spells with verbal components can't be cast while within the area of the sphere.

Disabling the Trap: The trap can be disabled by a successful DC 15 Arcana check. Alternatively, a Dispel Magic spell can negate the enchantment.

Alcove 2

Occupants: Thaelis the Illusionist and Baelgor the Pyromancer.

Conversation: Thaelis and Baelgor debate the destructive capabilities of the Rift Shard. Thaelis, with a hint of nostalgia in his eyes, wonders whether the Shard could be used to return to the days when his illusion magic was seen as a delight rather than a threat. On the other hand, Baelgor, with a determined set to his jaw, speculates that if used incorrectly, the Shard could escalate the eradication of magic, emphasizing the need for the Resistance to secure it at all costs. The two will add that they have heard that the Rift Shard is located in the Iron Conclave Fortress in a room known as The Shatter Room.

Trap Name: Illusionary Wall

Description: This trap, protecting the second alcove, is an illusory spell that disguises the alcove entrance as a solid stone wall.

Effect if Triggered: If a player walks into the illusionary wall, they pass through unharmed but alert the occupants of their presence.

Disabling the Trap: A successful DC 15 Investigation check reveals the wall's true nature. A Dispel Magic or True Seeing spell will also remove the illusion.

Alcove 3

Occupants: Neris the Enchanter and Zephyr the Aeromancer.

Conversation: Neris and Zephyr are engrossed in a detailed discussion about the implications of the Rift Shard's use. Neris muses about how the Shard's ability to create an antimagic field could provide safe havens for those terrified of magic's unpredictability. Meanwhile, Zephyr is keen on exploring the Shard's capability to fuel their spells, especially in critical situations where their magic could influence the course of the conflict against the Iron Conclave. They have heard rumor that the Rift Shard is in the Iron Conclave Fortress and wonder why the Iron Conclave is holding on to the Rift Shard.

Trap Name: Glyph of Warding

Description: This trap is an inscribed glyph that explodes when triggered, located at the entrance of the third alcove.

Effect if Triggered: The glyph is set to explode when a non-magic user steps within its radius. It deals 5d8 force damage to all within a 20-foot radius.

Disabling the Trap: The glyph can be found if the disarmer can see invisible objects. The glyph is invisible and can only be spotted by someone with See Invisibility, True Seeing or Detect Magic. The glyph trap can be disarmed with a Dispel Magic spell, or potentially with enough magical damage to destroy the glyph--although the latter will almost certainly alert everyone with the noise, unless a Silence spell or some other factor is in place.

Alcove 4

Occupants: Empty

Trap Name: Grappling Shadow

Description: This trap, protecting the fourth alcove, is an enchantment that causes shadows to animate and grasp at intruders.

Effect if Triggered: The animated shadows attempt to grapple any non-magic user who enters the alcove, restraining them. The player can use an action to make a DC 15 Strength (Athletics) check, escaping on a success.

Disabling the Trap: The trap can be disabled by a successful DC 15 Arcana check or a casting of the Dispel Magic spell.

The inclusion of the Rift Shard in these discussions reveals its importance to the Underground Resistance and offers Characters different perspectives on its potential uses and implications. The players can choose to join the conversation, gather information, or quietly listen in, depending on their alignment and mission objectives.

Additional Tasks

If the characters talk to Sorcerer Elandra, she will give them the following tasks:

Safe Passage: The Resistance needs to move a group of magic users, Ethereal Glade, through the Undercity to safety. The party is entrusted to escort them, ensuring they pass unharmed through the maze of tunnels and past any Iron Conclave patrols and bring them to Elandra.

Magical Cache Recovery: A hidden cache of magical items has been stashed in the Undercity, but its location has been lost. The party is asked to find and retrieve these items before the Iron Conclave does.

Subterranean Sabotage: The Resistance has learned of an impending Iron Conclave raid on the Undercity. The party is tasked with setting up traps and ambushes to slow down or halt the Iron Conclave's advance.

NPCs

Sorcerer Elandra: Elandra was a mage student at the time of The Shattering, narrowly escaping the disaster. Witnessing the devastation of magic misuse, she vowed to restore a balance where magic is understood and accepted, not feared. She now leads the Resistance with grace and optimism, a beacon of hope in the dark times.

Elowen the Green: A druid who was once at peace with nature before the Shattering disrupted her magical balance. She seeks to restore harmony between magic and the natural world.

Thaelis the Illusionist: A former entertainer whose illusion magic was considered harmless fun until it was outlawed. He fights to regain the freedom to express himself through his magic.

Baelgor the Pyromancer: A fire mage who was vilified for his destructive magic. He joined the Resistance to prove that even destructive magic could be used for good when in the right hands.

Neris the Enchanter: A scholar of enchantment magic who saw the potential for magic to bring joy and aid. She seeks to fight against the notion that all magic is dangerous.

Zephyr the Aeromancer: Once a weather mage who helped control the climate for crops, he wants to demonstrate the everyday helpfulness of magic.

Each of these characters provides different perspectives on magic, demonstrating that it isn't inherently good or evil, but a tool that depends on its user. They're united in their desire to restore a world where magic is understood and respected, not feared.

The Veilway

A treacherous path through the Undercity where The Unraveled gather.

The Veilway is a long, winding tunnel bathed in an ethereal gloom. Shimmering glyphs and symbols carved into the rough stone walls emit a faint, pulsating glow, providing the only source of light. The tunnel is shrouded in a mystical haze, causing the surroundings to blur and distort, turning the path into a dizzying array of warped images. The air is heavy with the scent of old, damp stone and the unplaceable, electrifying aroma of lingering magic.

Along the path, your party will see the Unraveled, their bodies flickering and shifting, their forms oscillating between reality and the arcane. Their presence is unnerving, the air around them shimmering as though warped by intense heat, making the atmosphere tense and charged.

The Veilway is an eerie and treacherous path within the Undercity, a perfect setting to test the courage and cunning of your adventurers. The Unraveled are both the opponents and the tragic embodiments of the danger of uncontrolled magic, a strong reminder of the perils of the post-Shattering world.

Bear in mind that this encounter is designed to challenge the party tactically and morally. The Unraveled are dangerous, but they are also victims. How the party chooses to engage them should be a reflection of their values and their current allegiances.

Conflict with The Unraveled

While navigating through the Veilway, the party's activities might attract the attention of The Unraveled, whose keen sense for magic and disturbances within the Undercity allows them to track the party. This could manifest as the Unraveled appearing when the group tries to disable the magical ward protecting the Gloves, or even when the party is attempting to interact with or disable the various magical traps in the area.

Determining the number of The Unraveled that interact with the Characters can depend on several factors:

Party Size: Consider the size of the party. As a general rule, you could start with a one-to-one ratio of Unraveled to party members. This ensures a balanced encounter that won't overwhelm the party but also won't be too easy.

Party Level: The level of the party should also be taken into account. Higher level parties can handle more Unraveled or a few stronger ones. For example, if the party level is high, consider adding a couple of Unraveled who have been in the Undercity longer and have more potent magic.

Current Situation: The party's actions in the Undercity can also influence the number of Unraveled. If they've been actively disrupting the magic in the area or have been making a lot of noise, more Unraveled might be drawn to their location.

Roll of the Dice: If you prefer leaving things to chance, you can roll a die to determine the number of Unraveled. For example, you might roll a d6, and the result could be the number of Unraveled that show up. This method adds an element of unpredictability, reflecting the chaotic nature of the Unraveled.

The Unraveled are unpredictable and may initially observe the group from a distance, phasing in and out of the ethereal plane. They might react aggressively if they perceive the group as a threat to the Undercity or to magic itself. This could occur if the group is openly displaying symbols of the Iron Conclave, wielding anti-magic artifacts, or attempting to destroy or disrupt the magical traps in the Veilway.

Additionally, The Unraveled are drawn to the use of magic, especially in large quantities or powerful spells. Any spellcasting in the Veilway might attract an Unraveled or even a group of them, leading to a potential conflict if they perceive the spellcasting as a threat or a misuse of magic.

Finally, any attempts to retrieve or interact with the Gloves of the Unraveled will certainly provoke a response. The Unraveled are strongly tied to these gloves, and they will do whatever they can to protect this powerful magical artifact.

Remember, The Unraveled are chaotic and highly protective of the Undercity and magic in general. They're not inherently evil, but their unpredictable nature and commitment to protect magic at all costs makes them formidable and unstable opponents. It has been a decade since the events of The Shattering and many of the Unraveled are insane. They're just as likely to engage in combat as they are to phase away if they feel outmatched, only to return later with reinforcements.

Consider this when creating a conflict with them, as it's not just about fighting but about navigating the volatile nature of their behavior. This creates a complex and unique challenge for the party, demanding both combat skills and strategic problem-solving.

Finding the Gloves of The Unraveled

As the adventurers progress through the Veilway, they may notice a dim glow emanating from a hidden alcove. This alcove can be discovered with a successful DC 15 Perception or Investigation check. The glow is partially obscured by an ethereal mist, a common feature in the Veilway, hinting at something magical within.

Inside the alcove, partially buried beneath rubble and old remnants of the Undercity, they will find the Gloves of the Unraveled. These gloves seem to constantly shift in color and texture, much like the Unraveled themselves, as if not entirely present in reality.

However, the gloves are guarded by a magical ward which can be detected with a DC 15 Investigation check, a final protective measure put in place by their last owner, an Unraveled who lost control over their magic. A successful DC 15 Arcana check will reveal the nature of the ward: it is an alarm spell that will summon an Unraveled if disturbed.

The adventurers will need to disarm the ward before they can safely retrieve the gloves. This can be done with a successful DC 17 Dexterity check (using Thieves' Tools). Alternatively, if the character is proficient in Arcana, they can instead choose to make an Intelligence (Arcana) check to disarm the trap. It can also be disarmed with Dispel Magic or a similar magic-removing effect.

In the case of a failed check, or if the adventurers decide to just grab the gloves, the alarm triggers, and an Unraveled phases into existence, ready to protect its possession. Once the Unraveled is dealt with, the gloves can be retrieved safely.

The Gloves of the Unraveled are an exceptional magic item that will greatly assist the adventurers in their journey, particularly in an environment as volatile as the Undercity. However, finding and retrieving them should be a challenging and exciting part of their journey.

For Characters Aligned with the Iron Conclave

The task at hand is clear: traverse the Veilway and neutralize The Unraveled, minimizing the magical influence within the Undercity. The Unraveled represent the dangers of unchecked magic, strengthening the resolve of those determined to eradicate such a volatile force.

For Characters Aligned with the Underground Resistance

The Veilway is a chilling testament to the danger of magic when it's not in balance, an example of the catastrophic outcome the Resistance is working to prevent. The Unraveled are a poignant reminder that these individuals need help, not condemnation, and that the path to restoring balance is more important than ever.

Lair Actions

On initiative count 20 (losing all initiative ties), the Veilway can take a lair action to cause one of the following magical effects; the Veilway can't use the same effect two rounds in a row:

Arcane Echo: The glyphs on the walls flare up, and the Veilway casts an echo of a spell previously cast in this combat by any creature, targeting a random opponent.

Unravel Reality: The Veilway distorts space within a 20-foot-radius sphere centered on a point it can see. The area is difficult terrain, and any creature inside must make a DC 15 Dexterity saving throw or take 2d6 force damage from the reality warp.

Phantasmal Resurgence: An Unraveled that was defeated rises again with 1 hit point, its form pulling itself together for one last stand. It disintegrates into arcane dust after 1 round.

Monster
The Unraveled

Reward
The Gloves of The Unraveled

Labyrinthine Depths

The most convoluted part of the Undercity, a maze-like network of tunnels and chambers, whose confusing layout has led many astray. It is perfect for the "Strategic Mapping" task.

The Labyrinthine Depths is a dizzying maze of tunnels and chambers, spiraling and splitting off in every direction. The walls, floor, and ceiling are made of a mixture of old bricks and natural stone, aged and worn down over time. Moss and other hardy fungi grow in patches, adding an earthy scent to the damp, cool air of the underground. The only light comes from the occasional phosphorescent fungi, creating an eerie, low-light atmosphere throughout the depths. Strange, echoing sounds bounce off the walls, making it hard to determine their source or distance.

This encounter is designed to challenge the players' navigational skills and their ability to handle elusive and unpredictable opponents. The maze-like layout of the Labyrinthine Depths and the ethereal nature of the Nexus Wisps are meant to keep the players on their toes and test their ability to adapt to unusual combat environments.

Solving the Maze

While the players are trying to solve the maze, the Nexus Wisps should add an extra layer of challenge, appearing at strategic moments to keep the tension high. Here's a potential system for their appearances:

Start: As the players begin to navigate the maze, introduce a single Nexus Wisp. This will serve to show the players what they're up against and gives them a chance to learn the Wisps' abilities.

Quarter Way: Once the players have made it a quarter of the way through the maze, introduce another Wisp. If they have managed to avoid or pacify the first one, this could be the first real combat encounter.

Halfway: At the halfway point, introduce two more Wisps. If the players are taking too long, this can serve as a motivator to speed up their progress. The Wisps should use hit-and-run tactics, using their Ethereal Burst and then retreating.

Three Quarters: Once the players are three-quarters of the way through, have a Wisp follow them. This Wisp doesn't attack, but its presence should keep the players on edge. It could potentially be used to foreshadow a larger encounter or another obstacle.

End: As the players reach the end of the maze, they encounter a final group of Wisps. There should be as many Wisps as players, forming the most challenging encounter yet.

Remember, the goal of the Wisps is not to defeat the players, but to harry and challenge them. They should primarily serve to create tension and urgency, distracting the players from the maze and forcing them to multitask. If a combat encounter seems to be dragging on or becoming too easy, don't be afraid to have a Wisp retreat or introduce a new one to keep things interesting.

Complex Maze

Standard Maze

clues or opportunities to use their magic to pacify or avoid the wisps, or even harness the energy of the wisps to stabilize the labyrinth.

Lair Actions

On initiative count 20 (losing initiative ties), the Labyrinthine Depths can take a lair action to cause one of the following magical effects:

Spatial Distortion: The labyrinth shifts and twists. Until the next lair action, the layout of the labyrinth changes, possibly separating the party or leading them into dead ends.

Magic Echo: The magic energies in the labyrinth amplify, causing all spells to echo. Until the next lair action, any spell cast within the labyrinth is automatically cast a second time at the original target. This can be both a boon and a danger, depending on the spell.

Wisp Surge: The Nexus Wisps respond to a surge of magic energy in the labyrinth. Two Nexus Wisps appear at locations chosen by the DM and act as allies of the existing wisps.

Monster

Nexus Wisp

Ethereal Glade

An enchanted glen filled with luminous flora and fauna, tucked away in the middle of the Undercity. The glowing plants here are remnants of ancient, magical ecosystems. The "Safe Passage" task could involve leading a group of nature-loving magic users who wish to study or find solace in this mystical environment.

As you journey deeper into the Undercity, the claustrophobic tunnels give way to an open space filled with a soft, ethereal glow. Vibrant fungi and plants, their colors ranging from cerulean blue to deep, luminescent purple, illuminate the glade. The air carries a sweet, intoxicating scent, and a soft hum of magical energy resonates around you. The leaves of the plants shimmer as they gently sway in an unseen breeze. You see soft, glowing orbs floating lazily through the air - wisps that blink in and out of existence. Despite being underground, the place feels alive, pulsing with a serene, otherworldly energy. The ground is soft beneath your feet, a mixture of luminescent moss and rich, fertile soil.

For Characters Aligned with the Iron Conclave

For characters aligned with the Iron Conclave, this encounter is a stark reminder of the chaos magic can cause. They see the Nexus Wisps as an embodiment of the unpredictable and destructive potential of magic and will likely seek to eradicate them. To highlight this, you can emphasize how the wisps seem to feed off the wild magic present in the labyrinth, potentially causing spatial distortions or other chaotic effects.

For Characters Aligned Underground Resistance

Characters aligned with the Underground Resistance may see the Nexus Wisps as unfortunate victims of The Shattering, innocent creatures that simply try to survive in this post-apocalyptic world. They might seek to find a way to safely navigate the labyrinth without causing harm to the wisps. To aid them, the DM could provide

This encounter provides an opportunity to showcase the beauty and wonder of magic in a world where it has been largely feared or rejected. As the players escort the nature-loving magic users through the Ethereal Glade, they'll witness a magical ecosystem that remains untouched by the chaos of the outside world. The effects of The Shattering were far and wide, but certain areas, such as the Undercity, were protected as they were far below ground. The enchanting environment can create a serene yet otherworldly ambiance to the scene. However, don't forget to remind your players that even the most captivating places in the Undercity can also harbor danger. Luminous flora and fauna might not be as benign as they appear, and the magical energies that permeate this area could give rise to unexpected effects or creatures.

For Characters Aligned with the Iron Conclave

Characters allied with the Iron Conclave may view this place as a dangerous concentration of uncontrolled magic. They may want to guide the group quickly through the glade to avoid unnecessary exposure to magic. They could also view the scholars as potential informants or assets in their efforts to control and eradicate magic.

For Characters Aligned Underground Resistance

For Characters allied with the Underground Resistance, this place is a haven, a symbol of what they are fighting for. They may wish to spend more time here, helping the scholars collect samples or study the magical flora and fauna. They could also see this as an opportunity to convince more magic users to join their cause.

Nature-Loving Magic Users

Eilinora Leafwhisper: A middle-aged elven druid who is fascinated by magical ecosystems and believes that studying them could bring about a new era of harmony between magic and nature. She once lived in a forest heavily imbued with magic and has been searching for a similar connection ever since she was driven into the Undercity.

Oris Thistleborne: A gnome wizard with an eccentric personality and a deep passion for magical botany. He is looking for new flora to add to his personal greenhouse in the Undercity, hoping that studying them will yield magical innovations that could benefit the city above.

Tarron Wildmane: A human ranger who used to patrol the wild magical zones in the city above. He has since become a guide in the Undercity, using his survival skills and knowledge of magical creatures to help others navigate the treacherous environment.

Original Fungi and Their Magical Properties

Edible Fungi for cooking

Honeyglow Puff: A rich, golden fungus that smells of honey and fresh earth. This sweet-tasting mushroom is often used in Undercity culinary dishes for its unique flavor.

Bluecap Button: A small, firm, and intensely flavorful mushroom, highly prized by Undercity cooks. These are often sautéed and added to stews or used to flavor local breads.

Veilvine: Resembling thin, trailing vines covered in delicate, edible fronds, Veilvine is often used as a garnish but can be consumed on its own. It has a subtle, earthy taste that pairs well with the robust flavors of the Undercity cuisine.

Beneficial Fungi

Aurora Cap: A mushroom that glows with a soft light, changing colors gently over time. When consumed, it provides the effect of the 'Darkvision' spell for 1 hour.

Pulse Pod: This bioluminescent fungus beats like a heart. When crushed and smeared on a weapon, the weapon is considered magical for the purpose of overcoming resistance and immunity to nonmagical attacks and damage for 1 hour.

Phantom Morel: This elusive fungus phases in and out of visibility. When consumed, it grants the user advantage on Stealth checks for 1 hour.

Blink Puffball: This mushroom releases a cloud of glowing spores when disturbed. When inhaled, it provides the effect of the 'Misty Step' spell, allowing a single use at will within the next minute.

Stardust Truffle: This rare, sparkling fungus grows deep within the glade. When consumed, it restores 1d4 expended spell slots, as if the user had completed a short rest.

Poisonous Fungi

Blightshade: A deep purple mushroom that exudes a sickly sweet smell. When consumed, the eater must make a DC 14 Constitution saving throw or take 2d4 poison damage and become poisoned for 1 hour.

Screaming Fungi: This mushroom appears harmless, but when touched, it emits a high-pitched scream that alerts nearby creatures and can cause temporary deafness. Those within 10 feet must succeed on a DC 15 Constitution saving throw or be deafened for 1 minute.

Torpor Spore: This grey-brown mushroom grows in dense clusters. When disturbed, it releases a cloud of spores in a 10-foot radius. Those who inhale the spores must make a DC 13 Constitution saving throw or fall unconscious for 1d4 rounds.

Crimson Wretch: This vivid red mushroom is highly toxic. If consumed, the eater must succeed on a DC 16 Constitution saving throw or take 2d6 poison damage initially and 1d6 poison damage at the start of each of their turns until they succeed on the saving throw.

Lair Actions

On initiative count 20 (losing initiative ties), the Ethereal Glade takes a lair action to cause one of the following magical effects; the glade can't use the same effect two rounds in a row:

Bioluminescent Burst: A cluster of the glowing flora suddenly bursts with a blinding light. Each creature within a 30-foot radius must succeed on a DC 15 Constitution saving throw or be blinded until the end of its next turn.

Fungal Bloom: A large patch of the ground erupts with rapidly growing fungi. The area becomes difficult terrain until cleared, and any creature that starts its turn in this area must succeed on a DC 15 Constitution saving throw or become poisoned until the end of its next turn as they inhale the toxic spores.

Ethereal Wisps: A swarm of ethereal wisps materialize and move through a space within the glade, distracting and obscuring vision. They create a heavily obscured area in a 20-foot radius for one round.

The Vault

An ancient burial vault repurposed as a storage space for magical items. It is hidden behind layers of illusion magic and is the goal for the "Magical Cache Recovery" task.

The vault is vast and filled with shelves upon shelves of artifacts, all cloaked in a sombre, silent atmosphere. Items of all shapes and sizes are scattered around, some on pedestals, some in glass cases, and some just left carelessly on the stone floor. A thin layer of dust coats everything, adding to the sense of timelessness that permeates the room. The faint hum of residual magic hangs in the air, filling the space with a sense of melancholy.

This encounter allows your players to explore a hidden and ancient vault filled with magical items, all of which have been affected by The Shattering. This could be a treasure trove for the party, but they should also proceed with caution. The illusions protecting the vault might not be the only defenses in place, and the damaged magical items could be unpredictable or dangerous. This encounter can serve as a fantastic opportunity to highlight the destructive impact of The Shattering on the world's magic.

For Characters Aligned with the Iron Conclave

For members of the Iron Conclave, the Vault of Echoes represents a dangerous collection of magic that needs to be contained or destroyed. Their goal could be to confiscate and neutralize these unpredictable magical items.

For Characters Aligned Underground Resistance

Those allied with the Underground Resistance might see this vault as a treasure trove of potential tools and weapons in their fight to stabilize magic. They might want to take as many items as they can, hoping to repair or repurpose them. They could also be interested in the vault itself, seeing it as a secure place to store their own magical items or as a base of operations.

Damaged Magical Items

Crystal of the Endless Void (Damaged): Originally designed as a Ring of Spell Storing, the Crystal of the Endless Void has been damaged and now functions unpredictably. When used to cast a stored spell, there's a 20% chance that a random spell (of equal or lesser level) is cast instead. Requires attunement.

Eternal Flame Torch (Damaged): This torch, previously an Everburning Torch, now functions sporadically due to damage. There is a 15% chance each hour that the flame extinguishes itself and will not relight for the next hour. Additionally, there's a 10% chance each hour that it suddenly flares up, providing bright light in a 60-foot radius and dim light for an additional 60 feet for one minute.

Ring of the Phantom (Damaged): Once a Ring of Invisibility, this damaged ring now functions inconsistently. When the wearer attempts to turn invisible, roll a d20. On a 1-5, the ring fails to activate. On a 16-20, the wearer becomes only semi-transparent, giving advantage on Stealth checks but not granting total invisibility. Requires attunement.

Armor of the Guardian Golem (Damaged): This was once a suit of Animated Armor, but now it has a mind of its own. Every hour the wearer must succeed on a DC 12 Charisma saving throw or the armor makes a random movement against their will (GM's discretion). Requires attunement.

Scepter of the Stormcaller (Damaged): Once capable of casting Control Weather, this damaged scepter now has a small, harmless cloud constantly hovering over it. Each time the wielder attempts to cast a spell, roll a d20. On a roll of 1, it instead casts Fog Cloud centered on the caster. Requires attunement.

Lair Actions

On initiative count 20 (losing initiative ties), the Vault of Echoes can exert its residual magical energy to cause one of the following effects; the vault can't use the same effect two rounds in a row:

Arcane Eruption: A random magical item in the vault releases a burst of magical energy. Each creature within a 20-foot radius must succeed on a DC 15 Dexterity saving throw or take 3d6 force damage.

Illusionary Guardians: The vault creates illusions of spectral warriors that move to attack intruders. Each creature in the vault must succeed on a DC 15 Intelligence (Investigation) check or be convinced of the illusions' reality, treating them as real threats until proven otherwise.

Magical Dampening Field: The vault generates a field of energy that suppresses magic. For 1 round, all magic items in the vault lose their magical properties.

The Iron Gate

A large, fortified entrance into the Undercity used by Iron Conclave patrols. The Resistance would want to sabotage this critical point to slow or halt an impending raid, as part of the "**Subterranean Sabotage**" task.

The Iron Gate stands as a stark, cold testament to the might of the Iron Conclave, a hulking metal monolith looming over the entryway into the Undercity. Its formidable structure is composed of a dark, corrosion-resistant alloy, adorned with severe, angular motifs that give it an imposing, ominous air. Scorch marks and old dents hint at previous unsuccessful attempts to breach it. High above, on adjacent ramparts, figures of armored Conclave guards can be seen, and the faint spectral shimmer of Echo Hounds prowling.

The Iron Gate encounter is about conflict with the Iron Conclave, stealth, and strategic sabotage. Consider having the encounter take place during an Iron Conclave patrol, introducing urgency and a living clock. The Echo Hounds patrol the area, making invisibility and quiet movement essential. Parties should consider a multi-pronged approach: distractions, diversions, and carefully timed actions could be key to successful sabotage.

For Characters Aligned with the Iron Conclave

To members of the Iron Conclave, the Iron Gate represents a vital defensive line against the forces of magic. They might be tasked with reinforcing its defenses or rooting out Resistance members plotting its sabotage. An encounter might involve facing the Underground Resistance, unearthing and disarming their sabotage attempts, or even hunting down Echo Hounds that have turned rogue.

For Characters Aligned Underground Resistance

For Resistance members, this gate is a symbol of their oppressors and a significant target. The aim could be to weaken the Iron Conclave's hold on the Undercity, causing enough chaos for a full-scale attack, or merely buying precious time for other Resistance plans. Successfully sabotaging the gate could involve stealthy infiltration, setting explosive magic runes, or turning Echo Hounds against their masters using magic.

Access to the Iron Conclave Fortress

The Iron Gate is not merely a physical gate; it is a sprawling checkpoint, a series of guarded chambers, and a labyrinth of corridors, creating an imposing and effective barrier to the fortress. The Gate is continuously manned by Conclave soldiers and their Echo Hounds. If the party can convincingly pose as Conclave members or others with legitimate access, they could potentially bypass the initial guards without resorting to combat.

Lower Level: The Undercity Access: Upon entering the gate, a long descending stairway leads to the lower level, providing access to the Undercity. Here, the party will encounter guards, transport personnel, and perhaps even prisoners being transported. Deception will be crucial as there are often higher-ranking Conclave officers overseeing operations. A forged order, well-crafted lie, or distraction could allow the party to proceed deeper into the fortress.

Surface-Level: The Courtyard and Main Fortress: Emerging from the fortress's underbelly, the party would find themselves in the courtyard within the fortress walls. The primary fortress building is a hive of activity, with Conclave officers, administrative personnel, and servants moving about. While not as guarded as the command center, maintaining their cover here is paramount to avoid raising an alarm.

Ultimately, the party's ability to move through the fortress will depend on their creativity, the strength of their deceptions, and their ability to adapt on the fly. Be prepared to improvise as the party interacts with the fortress's inhabitants and responds to challenges you did not anticipate.

Echo Hound Patrol

An Echo Hound Patrol refers to a group of Echo Hounds (usually 2-5, depending on the importance of the area being patrolled) alongside Iron Conclave soldiers (again, the number can vary based on the location's strategic importance).

The Echo Hounds, due to their invisibility and their ability to perceive their surroundings through sound, serve as the main scout and early warning system. They can detect incoming threats with their keen hearing, alerting their human handlers through specific sonic cues.

Iron Conclave soldiers accompanying the Echo Hounds are trained to interpret these cues and react accordingly. These soldiers carry specialized equipment - often magic-dampening weaponry and gear designed to protect against magical effects.

Patrol routes are typically set to cover the most vulnerable or vital areas, with the Echo Hounds ranging slightly ahead of their handlers. The timing of patrols might vary, with some occurring on a regular schedule while others might be more random to prevent predictability.

In combat, the Echo Hounds serve as the first line of defense, using their Sonic Screech to disorient and damage enemies. The soldiers follow up, moving in to neutralize threats while they're stunned or disoriented.

It's worth noting that Echo Hound patrols, due to the nature of the creatures, are almost silent. They might be upon the adventurers before they realize it, particularly in the echoing chambers of the Undercity. This makes them a deadly and efficient tool in the Iron Conclave's arsenal.

Lair Actions

At initiative count 20 (losing all ties), the Iron Conclave can trigger one of the following lair actions, provided there are Conclave Guards within the lair to execute them:

Gate Mechanisms Activation: The Conclave Guards activate the fortress gate's defensive mechanisms. Traps, such as arrow slits or magic-dampening fields, are triggered. Any creature within 20 feet of the gate must succeed on a DC 15 Dexterity saving throw or take 4d10 piercing damage from the sprung traps, or must succeed on a DC 15 Constitution saving throw or have their magic suppressed for one round (as if under the effects of an Antimagic Field spell).

Echo Hound Release: The Conclave Guards release an additional Echo Hound from the fortress kennels. This Echo Hound immediately rolls initiative and acts on its own turn.

Battlements Activation: Conclave Guards at the gate unleash a volley of arrows at their foes. Each enemy in sight and within range of the archers must succeed on a DC 15 Dexterity saving throw or take 4d8 piercing damage.

Monster

Echo Hounds

Conclave Guards

The Undercity Market

A clandestine gathering place for trading magical items and components.

The Undercity Market is a sight to behold. Picture a bustling, torch-lit bazaar that stretches out beneath a cavernous, stone ceiling, riddled with bioluminescent fungi that lend an otherworldly glow to the proceedings. Stalls carved into the rocky walls house a myriad of vendors, displaying an array of magical items, shimmering potions, and rare artifacts. Traders from all walks of life, some disguised to conceal their identities, haggle over prices and barter goods amidst the cacophony of the market.

Shadowy figures move between the stalls, exchanging hushed words and suspicious glances, a testament to the covert nature of this underground trade. The air is heavy with the smell of magic-infused incense and the tang of damp earth, while the ambient sound of hushed whispers, clinking coins, and the occasional argument fill the air.

The Undercity Market is a hub of activity and excitement, buzzing with vendors and customers who understand the risks and rewards of dealing in magical wares. It's a place where the Underground Resistance members can find important magical components or information, and where the Iron Conclave could disrupt a vital resource for the magical community. As such, it can serve as the backdrop for a variety of encounters, from covert negotiations and haggling to a full-blown confrontation.

For Characters Aligned with the Iron Conclave

For characters aligned with the Iron Conclave, the Undercity Market represents a significant blow to the Resistance. It's a chance to seize illegal magical items, apprehend traders, and gain information on the Resistance. A stealthy approach could lead to successful infiltration, allowing them to gather intelligence or plant false information. Alternatively, they could plan a raid to capture the market vendors, hoping to disrupt the Resistance's supply chain.

For Characters Aligned Underground Resistance

For characters in the Underground Resistance, the Market offers valuable resources and allies. They could be there to procure much-needed magical items, to seek information, or to protect the traders from the Conclave. Ensuring the market's security could involve rooting out spies, reinforcing protective enchantments around the market, or arranging safe passage for key traders.

Undercity Market Vendors

Varis the Veiled

Varis is a mysterious figure who deals exclusively in magical artifacts. Cloaked and masked, his identity remains unknown. His merchandise varies from ancient scrolls and arcane relics to mystical talismans.

Name	Description	Properties	Price (GP)
Chronal Fragment	A shard from a shattered timepiece. Pulses with temporal energy	As an action, user can shatter the fragment to take an additional turn immediately, but ages 1d10 years. One-time use.	500
Veil of Varis	A mask that shimmers with illusion magic	User can cast 'Alter Self' once per day without expending a spell slot.	700
Soul Lantern	An ethereal lantern which reveals spectral entities	When lit, the user can see into the Ethereal Plane within a 30 foot radius. Burns for 1 hour.	300
Understone Amulet	An amulet embedded with a stone from the Undercity, glows faintly with protective magic	User gains resistance to poison damage and advantage on saving throws against being poisoned.	600

Sundry Stuffs

This stall, managed by an old gnome named Brickleburr, offers a variety of adventuring gear adapted for the Undercity - waterproof torches, rope resistant to acidic Undercity slimes, and maps of ever-shifting tunnels.

Name	Description	Properties	Price (GP)
Waterproof Torch	A specially treated torch that doesn't go out when exposed to water	Functions as a regular torch, but remains lit even underwater or in heavy rain. Lasts for 1 hour.	5
Acid-Resistant Rope	A 50-ft length of rope treated to resist corrosive substances	Functions as a regular rope, but is not damaged by acid.	10
Glow Moss Lantern	A lantern filled with luminous moss that casts a soft green glow	Casts bright light in a 15-foot radius and dim light for an additional 15 feet. Can be refueled with Glow Moss.	25
Slimeproof Boots	Sturdy leather boots treated with a slime-resistant compound	The wearer gains advantage on Dexterity saving throws to avoid slipping or falling due to slimes or other slippery substances in the Undercity.	30

Ethereal Enchantments

Operated by a pair of half-elf sisters, Elysia and Lyria, this stall specializes in enchanted jewelry. They offer rings of darkvision, amulets for poison resistance, and other trinkets enchanted to help survival in the Undercity.

Name	Description	Properties	Price (GP)
Ring of Undercity Senses	A simple silver ring that enhances the wearer's senses to adapt to the Undercity	The wearer gains advantage on Wisdom (Perception) checks relying on hearing or smell while in the Undercity.	200
Amulet of Vermin Friendship	A wooden amulet carved with the image of a rat	Beasts in the Undercity with a CR of 0 will not attack the wearer unless provoked.	150
Bracelet of Dark Whispers	A black onyx bracelet that whispers guidance to the wearer in the Undercity	The wearer can use an action to ask the bracelet for direction to the nearest exit, and it will lead the way. Usable once per long rest.	300
Earring of Echo Location	A small hoop earring that allows the wearer to perceive their surroundings through echolocation	The wearer gains blindsight out to a range of 10 feet.	350
Locket of Slime Resistance	A locket filled with a magically preserved petal from a rare Undercity flower	The wearer has resistance to acid damage.	400

Dusk Bloom Apothecary

Run by a soft-spoken tiefling called Vesh, this shop sells potions brewed from Undercity fungi and flora. From potions of healing to vials of bioluminescent light, Vesh has a cure, poison, or brew for most occasions.

Name	Description	Properties	Price (GP)
Potion of Fungi Healing	A potion made from unique Undercity fungi that speeds up healing	When consumed, regain 2d4+2 hit points and gain advantage on saving throws against disease for the next 24 hours.	50
Underlight Vial	A small vial filled with a bioluminescent substance	When cracked, the vial emits bright light in a 20-foot radius and dim light for an additional 20 feet. Lasts for 1 hour.	10
Venom of the Underbeast	A potent poison harvested from deadly creatures lurking in the Undercity	Can be applied to a weapon or ammunition. On a hit, the target takes an additional 1d6 poison damage and must make a DC 13 Constitution saving throw or be poisoned for 1 minute.	150
Elixir of Deep Sight	A potion brewed from Undercity plants	When consumed, gain darkvision out to a range of 60 feet for 1 hour.	60

| Bottle of Echo Essence | A potion that temporarily enhances one's auditory perception | When consumed, gain advantage on Wisdom (Perception) checks that rely on hearing for 1 hour. | 30 |

Shard's Shiny Stones

Shard, a kobold with an eye for gems, runs a gambling game where customers bet on which of his trained cave lizards will return with the most valuable gem from a maze of tunnels. Winners can keep the gem their lizard returns with.

Name	Description	Properties	Price (GP)
Lustrous Lapis Lazuli	A deep blue semi-precious stone that seems to shimmer with an internal light.	Can be used as a focus for casting spells that deal cold damage. Increases the damage of such spells by 1.	100
Glowing Garnet	A red gem that glows softly in the dark.	Can be used as a focus for casting spells that deal fire damage. Increases the damage of such spells by 1.	100
Chameleon Chrysocolla	A vibrant gem that changes its color according to the bearer's mood.	Can be used as a focus for casting spells that manipulate emotions (like Charm Person). The DC of these spells increases by 1.	150
Thunderous Topaz	A bright yellow gem that sparks with electricity.	Can be used as a focus for casting spells that deal lightning damage. Increases the damage of such spells by 1.	100
Eye of the Underbeast	A rare black pearl with a smoky interior, said to be found only in the belly of Undercity beasts.	When used in crafting magic items, the DC to create the item decreases by 2.	500

Faelin's Phantom Phood

This food stall, run by a plump halfling named Faelin, offers ethereal meals that nourish both the body and the soul. His spectral stews are especially popular among spirits and spectral entities within the Undercity.

Name	Description	Properties	Price (GP)
Ghost Grog	A translucent ale that's as refreshing to spirits as it is to the living.	Restores 1d4 hit points to living creatures. To spectral entities, it restores 1d8 hit points.	10
Wraith Whisky	A strong, smoky drink, aged in ghostly oak barrels.	Imbibers gain advantage on saving throws against being frightened for 1 hour. For spectral entities, it also provides +2 to AC for the same duration.	20
Spectral Stew	A hearty, ethereal stew that fills and warms any soul.	Restores 1d8 hit points and the eater does not need to eat again for 24 hours. For spectral entities, it also grants advantage on all Constitution saving throws for the next 24 hours.	15

Phantom Pasty	A flaky, translucent pastry filled with spectral spiced meat.	Eater gains the benefits of a short rest. For spectral entities, this also restores all their hit points.	50
Ectoplasm Eclairs	These light, airy pastries are filled with a sweet, glowing cream.	Eater gains advantage on Charisma checks for the next hour. For spectral entities, the advantage lasts for 24 hours.	15

Whisper's Secrets

Whisper, an old and blindfolded tabaxi woman, deals in information. Secrets, rumors, or the latest gossip in the Undercity, she knows it all. For a price, she's willing to share.

Name	Description	Properties	Price (GP)
Hidden Pathways	Whisper knows secret routes through the Undercity.	Provides advantage on Survival checks when navigating the Undercity for one day.	50
Merchant's Schedule	Information about when certain vendors arrive and what they will sell.	Allows characters to access a specific vendor's goods at an opportune time, potentially before others.	25
Guard Patterns	Knowledge of the guard schedules and patterns at the Iron Gate.	Provides advantage on Stealth checks around the Iron Gate for one day.	75
Echo Hound Habitats	Information on where Echo Hounds typically reside and hunt.	Provides a bonus to Survival checks when trying to avoid Echo Hounds in the Undercity.	40
Forgotten Lore	Ancient stories and knowledge about the Undercity's past.	Provides a bonus to History or Arcana checks related to the Undercity.	60
Resistance Movements	The latest news on the Underground Resistance's plans and operations.	Grants the characters insider knowledge that could impact their strategy or next move.	100
Iron Conclave Secrets	Inside information about the Iron Conclave, including strategies, key players, and plans.	Characters gain a piece of useful information or secret about the Iron Conclave that can aid their mission.	150
Nexus Wisp Sightings	Recent sightings and habits of Nexus Wisps.	Provides advantage on checks to track or find Nexus Wisps in the Undercity for one day.	30
Shattered Item Locations	Clues to the location of magical items damaged in The Shattering.	Grants the characters a lead or hint towards finding a damaged magical item in the Undercity.	100

| Undercity Rumors | General gossip about goings-on in the Undercity. | Characters gain a piece of general knowledge or rumor that could be useful or interesting. | 20 |

The DM should take into account the party's current funds, their goals, and the ongoing plot when deciding which secrets Whisper might have available at any given time. The exact information provided by each "item" should be created by the DM to fit their campaign.

Blacksmith Albern

Albern is a man caught between two worlds - the love for his son, who has innate magic abilities, and his desire for order. He has aligned with the Iron Conclave in hopes to appease the new leaders and protect his son. If the characters approach Albern, he will give the following additional tasks to characters aligned to the Iron Conclave. For each task completed, he will reward the characters with one item from his Blacksmith shop.

Cryptic Infiltration: The Iron Conclave has received intelligence about a gathering of magic users within the depths of the Undercity. The players are tasked to infiltrate this gathering, capture or eliminate the magic users, and confiscate any magical items they may possess.

Trap Neutralization: The Resistance has filled the Undercity with numerous magical traps. The Iron Conclave assigns the players to disable these traps to make the Undercity safer for their patrols and to demonstrate the danger posed by unrestrained magic.

Strategic Mapping: The Undercity's tunnels are a convoluted labyrinth. The Iron Conclave needs a detailed map of the network to help them more effectively search for magic users. The party is tasked with exploring the Undercity and creating an accurate map.

Name	Description	Properties	Price (GP)
Resonating Sword	A sword infused with a unique metal that resonates when near magic.	Acts as a +1 Longsword. Additionally, it hums softly when within 30 feet of a source of magic.	300
Iron Ward Amulet	An amulet designed to protect the wearer from magical effects.	While wearing this amulet, you have advantage on saving throws against spells and other magical effects.	800
Shattering Hammer	A warhammer designed to disrupt magical fields and items.	Acts as a +1 Warhammer. On a hit, it can disrupt concentration on spells and might damage or temporarily deactivate magical items (DM's discretion).	350
Echo Arrowheads	Arrowheads crafted to make arrows more effective against Echo Hounds.	When used against Echo Hounds, arrows with these heads deal an extra 1d6 thunder damage.	100 for a set of 10
Stabilizing Gauntlets	Gauntlets designed to help control wild magic surges.	While wearing these gauntlets, a spellcaster can choose to reroll one roll on the Wild Magic Surge table, but they must use the new roll.	500
Undercity Compass	A special compass that points towards the nearest exit to the surface.	Acts as a compass in the Undercity, guiding the way to the nearest surface exit.	250
Warding Shield	A shield engraved with anti-magic runes.	Acts as a +1 Shield. Once per day, it can cast the Shield spell as a reaction without using a spell slot.	600

Lair Actions

On initiative count 20 (losing initiative ties), the Market takes a lair action to cause one of the following magical effects; the Market can't use the same effect two rounds in a row:

Camouflage: The myriad of magical items within the Market flare up, creating a dazzling light show that obscures the field of view. Until the next round, attack rolls against targets within the Market have disadvantage.

Alarmed Stalls: A stall owner activates a magical alarm, releasing a loud, disorientating noise that reverberates around the market. Each creature of the Market's choice within 60 feet of the activated stall must succeed on a DC 15 Wisdom saving throw or be frightened until the end of its next turn.

Mystical Feedback: The concentration of magic within the market spikes, causing a magical backlash. Each spellcaster within the Market must succeed on a DC 15 Constitution saving throw or take 2d6 psychic damage.

NPC

Blacksmith Albern

Reward

Items from Albern's Blacksmith shop

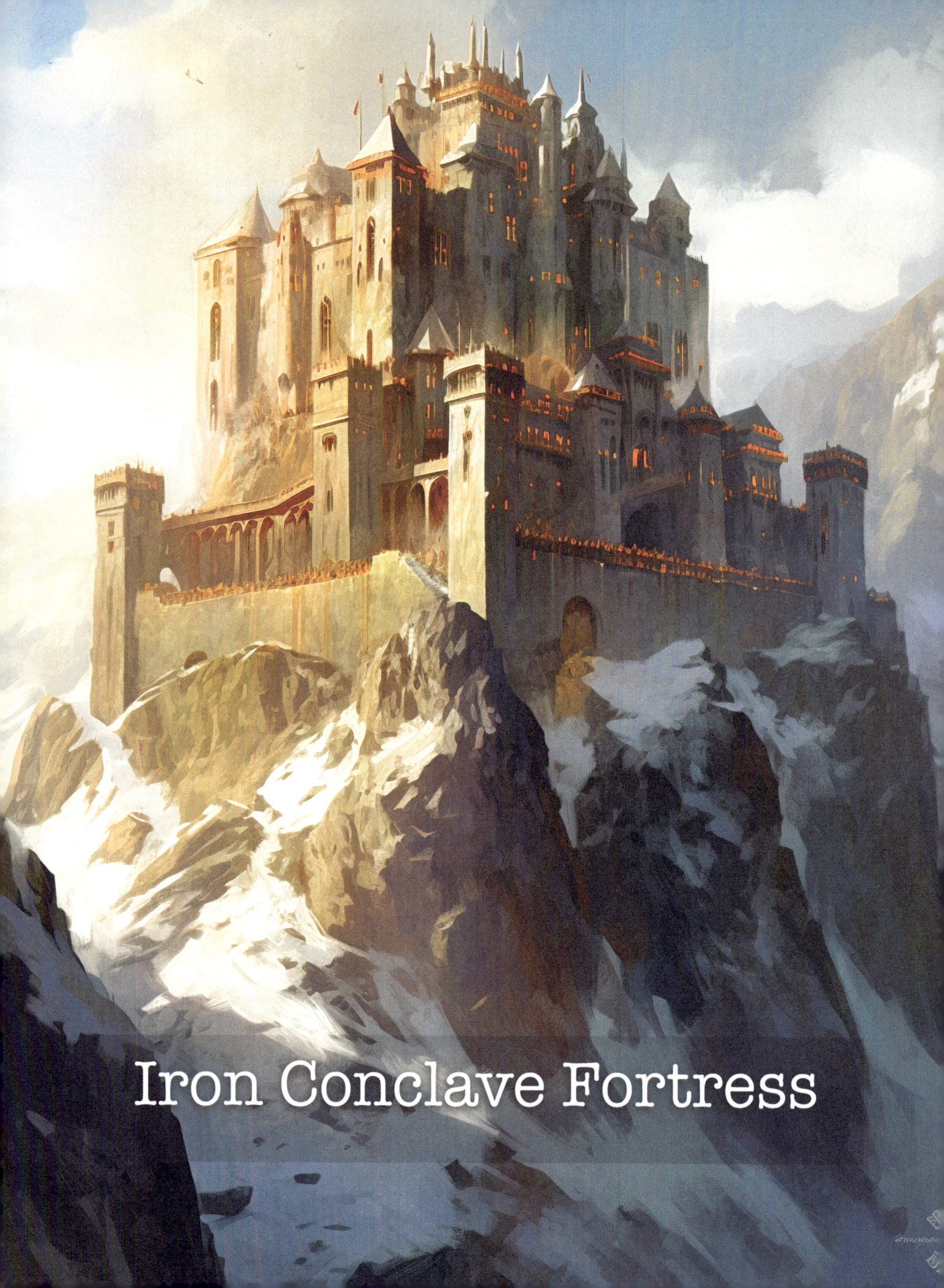

Iron Conclave Fortress

Iron Conclave Fortress

The Iron Conclave Fortress is a setting that reflects the militant and rigid mindset of its occupants. Its structures are built for functionality and defense, with an almost industrial aesthetic, contrasting the organic and chaotic environment of the Undercity. Within the fortress, the party will encounter Conclave Guards, Brutes, and Elites, along with the fortress's stern leader, Commander Gaius Tarn.

As you guide your players through this fortress, emphasize the cold and oppressive atmosphere, the strict order, and the ever-watchful eyes of the Iron Conclave. Their journey through the fortress should feel like an infiltration mission, filled with tense encounters and opportunities for stealth and subterfuge.

Keep in mind the ultimate goals of the party: the Resistance-aligned characters aim to find and extract the Rift Shard, while Iron Conclave-aligned characters plan to deliver the Shard to the Ritual Chamber to end all magic.

The tunnel leading from the Iron Gate in the Undercity to the Fortress opens up on the Courtyard grounds. Below the surface are stone stairs leading up to a hinged grate door with no lock that opens from either side. This grated door serves two purposes. For one, the grate appears to be a simple drain under all but the closest scrutiny. The tunnel also serves as an emergency escape route in case of a devastating attack or magical cataclysm, such as another Shattering.

Remember that the fortress is also a living, breathing location with soldiers going about their routines, and certain areas like the War Room and Barracks might provide interesting social interactions or opportunities for gathering information. In contrast, areas like the Shatter Room and Ritual Chamber are likely to be heavily guarded and warded, providing challenges that will test your players' skills and abilities.

A fortress as cold and unyielding as the ideology of those who inhabit it, the Iron Conclave Fortress is a formidable stronghold situated in the heart of the Iron Conclave's territory. From here, they plan their operations and strategies for the eradication of all magic, making it a significant location for the Resistance to infiltrate and disrupt.

Conclave Guard Patrols

The Iron Conclave places great emphasis on maintaining the security of their fortress, and as such, their guards are well-drilled and their patrols are meticulously planned. Here's an overview of how these patrols might operate:

Fortress Walls: On the fortress walls, four squads of five guards each patrol in a clockwise direction, starting from the main entrance. Each squad is positioned in such a way that when one squad is at a corner, the other squads are evenly spaced along the walls. This pattern ensures that all sections of the wall are always within sight of at least one squad. Patrol squads on the wall are changed every four hours.

Courtyard and Grounds: Two squads of six guards each patrol the grounds and courtyard of the fortress. One squad patrols the periphery while the other roams the central areas, including near important buildings and structures. These squads change every six hours. Each squad will also be accompanied by a Prohibition Construct.

Guardhouse: The guardhouse is always manned by a standing squad of five guards, changed every eight hours. One guard is always posted at the main entrance to the guardhouse, while the other three monitor the surveillance apparatus and respond to alerts from other parts of the fortress.

Strategic Locations (War Room, Shatter Room, Ritual Chamber): Each of these key locations has a dedicated team of four Conclave Guards (Brutes). These are guards chosen for their loyalty and proficiency. They remain on post for twelve-hour shifts, ensuring the most important locations in the fortress are well guarded at all times.

It's important to note that these patterns are maintained rigorously, creating predictable patterns that can be exploited. However, the Iron Conclave is not complacent - unexpected checks by commanding officers, the presence of Prohibition Constructs, and an always-ready quick response force ensure that breaching the fortress remains a daunting task.

An additional thing to remember is that any use of magic within the Fortress is likely to draw immediate attention and swift response from nearby patrols or the quick response force, making the use of magic a risky proposition in all but the most desperate circumstances.

The Guardhouse

This structure houses the guards that protect the entrance to the fortress. It contains armories, barracks, and possibly a hidden entrance to the fortress.

The Guardhouse is an imposing structure of cold grey stone, built to mirror the fortress's unyielding strength. The facade is dotted with narrow, barred windows that offer a glimpse into the military precision and discipline within. The hum of activity from within suggests a constant state of vigilance.

Inside, rows of neatly arranged bunk beds, a meticulously organized armory filled with polished weapons and shining armor, and a strategy table crowded with maps and parchments provide testament to the readiness of the Conclave's forces. In the heart of the Guardhouse, a hidden door - if discovered - leads to a secret passageway into the fortress, a clandestine vein running through the fortress's very heart.

The Guardhouse encounter is a chance for characters to interact with the Iron Conclave's military force directly. They may choose to infiltrate it, which can involve stealth or disguise, or they may confront the guards head-on. The presence of a potential hidden entrance into the fortress could offer a strategic advantage to the party, depending on how they discover and utilize it.

In the Guardhouse, there are 10 Conclave Guards present. They work in shifts - 5 are usually on active duty, while the other 5 rest or perform routine maintenance tasks. Note that if the alarm is raised, off-duty guards will be quick to join the fray.

Discovering the hidden entrance into the fortress requires a keen eye and a clever mind. Players can find clues hinting towards its location making a passive Insight check (DC15) for each clue:

Inconsistent architectural plans: If they find a blueprint or a sketch of the Guardhouse layout, they may notice that the Guardhouse is smaller on the inside than it appears from the outside, indicating a hidden space.

Out of place construction: A segment of the wall in the rest area of the Guardhouse is constructed with different, newer materials. This might be a hint to a recent construction - the secret door.

Hushed conversations: If a player overhears guards talking in hushed tones about the 'delivery door' or 'secret route', it might tip them off about the existence of a hidden passage.

Detecting the secret door will require a successful Perception or Investigation check (DC 15). If they have discovered clues, you could lower the DC or give them advantage on this check.

Upon entering the secret passage, it winds its way through the fortress's interior, bypassing many of the more public areas. It will bring them out into a small, lesser-known storeroom adjacent to the War Room. This will allow them to be closer to the strategic center of the fortress, providing an advantage for their mission.

For Characters Aligned with Iron Conclave

Characters in support of the Conclave's cause may find allies in the guards, extracting vital information about the fortress's defenses and the Conclave's plans. They could even persuade the guards to assist them in their quest for the Rift Shard, justifying it as a necessary measure for the eradication of magic.

For Characters Aligned with Underground Resistance

For those supporting the Underground Resistance, the Guardhouse presents a challenge to overcome. Stealth, distraction, or cunning might be used to infiltrate the armory, gain disguises, or find the hidden entrance. Confrontation isn't the only option; convincing a guard to question the Conclave's doctrine could sow the seeds of internal dissent.

Lair Actions

On initiative count 20 (losing initiative ties), the Guardhouse takes a lair action to cause one of the following effects; the Guardhouse can't use the same effect two rounds in a row:

The Guardhouse signals for reinforcements. Two additional guards emerge from the barracks, ready to defend their post.

An alarm bell is rung, alerting the entire fortress of intruders. All guards within the Guardhouse are now on high alert, making stealth nearly impossible without magical assistance.

The armory's defenses are triggered, causing a sudden barrier of thick iron bars to fall into place, separating the armory from the rest of the Guardhouse. Anyone inside the armory is now trapped unless they can find a way to lift the barrier.

Monster

Conclave Guards

The Courtyard

The Courtyard Encounter provides an excellent opportunity to showcase the intensity of the Iron Conclave's efforts to control magic and also the devastating effects of uncontrolled magic. The presence of the Reclaimed Dead in a cage is a grim reminder of the chaos caused by magic.

The encounter can be used as an investigation or combat encounter, depending on your party's alignment and the course of action they decide to take. Ranger Yoren, present in the Courtyard, could provide valuable information or assistance if approached correctly.

The Courtyard is a vast, open expanse within the fortress walls, dominated by grim grey cobblestone and flanked by intimidating, high stone walls. Here, under the watchful gaze of patrolling guards, Conclave soldiers train in disciplined formations, their rhythmic footsteps echoing against the stark stone.

At the far end of the Courtyard, a chilling sight awaits - a large, iron cage containing Reclaimed Dead. Their ethereal forms shimmer eerily under the watchful eyes of the Conclave guards, a harsh reminder of the devastating effects of uncontrolled magic. The mournful glow in their eyes is a haunting spectacle amidst the austere setting.

For Characters Aligned with Iron Conclave

For characters who wish to uphold the Conclave's goal of eradicating magic, this encounter could solidify their beliefs further. They may want to investigate the Reclaimed Dead, learning more about the horrific transformation, which could be used to rally support against magic use. Engaging with Ranger Yoren may provide more insight into the Conclave's strategies and plans.

For Characters Aligned with Underground Resistance

Those who wish to stabilize magic could see this encounter as a sobering reminder of their mission's urgency. Freeing the Reclaimed Dead could be an objective, not only as a compassionate act but also as a method to sow chaos within the fortress. Alternatively, they may want to engage with Ranger Yoren discreetly, gathering vital intelligence or securing a potential ally.

Lair Actions

On initiative count 20 (losing initiative ties), the Iron Conclave Fortress takes a lair action to cause one of the following effects; the fortress can't use the same effect two rounds in a row:

The fortress's defenses spring into action. Siege weapons atop the walls rotate and aim at a target of the fortress's choosing within range and sight, making a ranged attack (+7 to hit, range 200/800 ft., one target. Hit: 20 (3d10) piercing damage).

A group of Conclave guards, responding to a perceived threat, rush into the courtyard from one of the nearby buildings, potentially changing the dynamics of any ongoing engagements.

The fortress signals an alarm, causing bright, flashing arcane lights to flare up around the courtyard, making it difficult for intruders to remain unseen. All stealth checks are at a disadvantage until the next lair action.

Monster

Reclaimed Dead

Prohibition Constructs

Conclave Guards

NPC

Ranger Yoren

The War Room

The War Room is the strategic heart of the Iron Conclave's operations and is heavily guarded by 1d4 Conclave Guards (Brute). As such, getting in and out undetected will be a significant challenge. It will also be a potential treasure trove of information, particularly for characters aligned with the Underground Resistance.

The War Room is a large, imposing chamber with a large circular table at its heart. The walls are lined with bookcases filled with tomes, scrolls, and maps. Several strategic maps are pinned to the walls, illuminated by a soft, magical light. At the far end of the room, a large hearth crackles, casting dancing shadows around the room. The air is heavy with the smell of old parchment, burning wood, and a subtle undertone of magic.

For Characters Aligned with Iron Conclave

Characters aligned with the Iron Conclave may have an easier time gaining access to the War Room. They could be asked to attend a strategy meeting or report on recent findings. The intelligence gathered from the War Room can provide them with a broader perspective on the Conclave's plans and strategic positions, potentially affecting their decisions and actions moving forward.

For Characters Aligned with Underground Resistance

For characters aligned with the Underground Resistance, infiltrating the War Room can yield valuable intelligence about the Conclave's plans and operations. If they're clever and careful, they may be able to sabotage some of the Conclave's operations, or at least provide their allies with crucial information.

Maps and Documents

Fortress Blueprints: These provide a detailed layout of the Fortress, including guard patrols and trap placements. They could reveal a direct route to the Ritual Chamber or the Shatter Room.

Conclave Operation Plans: These documents outline upcoming Conclave operations aimed at suppressing magic use in nearby regions. This could provide the Resistance with an opportunity to interfere or prepare defenses.

Magical Artefact Inventories: A detailed account of magical artefacts that the Conclave has confiscated, their current locations within the Fortress, and notes on their properties. This could be useful in identifying potential tools or allies.

Ritual Notes: Scattered notes about the ritual intended to destroy magic. It might contain vital clues about how to prevent or reverse the ritual, or even what the Conclave's true intentions are.

Prisoner Records: Lists of magic-users detained by the Conclave, including their current location in the Fortress. This could be useful for characters looking to free these prisoners or use their help.

Letters from Commander Tarn: These personal letters from the commander might reveal weaknesses in the Conclave's operations, or hint at a way to negotiate or reason with him.

Lair Actions

On initiative count 20 (losing initiative ties), the room's defensive mechanisms activate. Select one of the following effects; the same effect can't be used two rounds in a row:

The room's lighting system suddenly brightens to a blinding intensity. Each creature in the room must succeed on a DC 15 Constitution saving throw or be blinded until the lair's next initiative count 20.

Reinforced steel shutters slam down over the room's entrances and exits. They remain sealed until the lair's next initiative count 20.

Hidden panels in the walls open up, and a barrage of harmless, but distracting, flash pellets are ejected into the room. Each creature in the room must succeed on a DC 15 Wisdom saving throw or be distracted and unable to focus, suffering disadvantage on attack rolls and ability checks until the lair's next initiative count 20.

Monster

Conclave Guard

Fortress Walls

The walls surrounding the fortress offer a panoramic view of the surrounding lands, but are also a dangerous place, patrolled by sentinels and defended by siege weaponry.

The walls of the Iron Conclave Fortress tower menacingly above, an unbroken line of cold stone that stretches as far as the eye can see. The top of the wall is dotted with watchtowers and adorned with banners bearing the emblem of the Iron Conclave, fluttering in the wind. At intervals along the wall, gargantuan siege weapons stand silent and imposing, ready to rain destruction upon any who dare to threaten the fortress.

This encounter is all about high stakes and careful planning. The party's approach will be greatly influenced by their alignment. Keep in mind the heightened sense of alertness among the Conclave Guards, the exposure due to the panoramic view, and the dangerous power of the siege weaponry. Introduce environmental challenges like gusts of wind, birds' nests, or loose stones that can betray the party's presence if disturbed.

For Characters Aligned with Iron Conclave

Players aligned with the Iron Conclave are familiar with the patterns of the patrol guards and can use this knowledge to their advantage. They can access the siege weapons, using their authority or disguise, to create a diversion or to fend off any attacks.

For Characters Aligned with Underground Resistance

Those aligned with the Resistance might choose to use stealth and subterfuge to navigate these dangerous heights. They could potentially sabotage the siege weapons or create a distraction elsewhere on the wall to draw guards away from their intended path.

Siege Weapon

One of the notable siege weapons is the Iron Conclave Ballista. This huge crossbow-like machine is capable of launching massive bolts over long distances, causing devastating damage. It takes a crew of three to operate efficiently - one to aim, one to load, and one to fire. When manned, it can launch a bolt up to 1200 feet, dealing 3d10 piercing damage on a hit. It's a threat to any incoming aerial or ground-based assault, a formidable testament to the might and engineering prowess of the Iron Conclave.

Lair Actions

On initiative count 20 (losing initiative ties), one of the wall's defensive mechanisms activates. The same effect can't be used two rounds in a row:

The wall's alarm bells start to ring loudly, alerting all creatures in the fortress. The noise continues until the lair's next initiative count 20.

A group of trained falcons is released from hidden compartments in the walls. They fly at the invaders, attempting to knock them off the wall or distract them. All creatures on the wall must make a DC 15 Dexterity saving throw or be knocked prone.

The siege weapons are activated, launching a barrage of stones into the sky that land around the fortress, creating a hazardous terrain. Anyone in the area must make a DC 15 Dexterity saving throw or take 4d10 bludgeoning damage from the falling debris.

Monster

Conclave Guards

The Shatter Room

This encounter is critical and should carry weight in terms of both tension and possible outcomes. Both groups will have vastly different goals regarding the Rift Shard. How they go about achieving these goals and the choices they make during the encounter could have significant implications for the future of the campaign.

The Shatter Room is well-protected. Direct assault might seem unwise and could lead to high casualties. Stealth, deception, or diplomacy could also play a part, depending on your party's approach. Keep in mind that Tarn is a strategic thinker - he will not be easily fooled and will use every resource at his disposal to protect the Rift Shard.

The Shatter Room is a fortress within a fortress, a domed chamber of cold iron and lead, designed to contain and suppress the raw, untamed power of the Rift Shard. The Shard, approximately 6 inches in length and weighing 4 pounds, itself is held aloft in the center of the room, within a cage of heavy iron bars, humming with energy and casting harsh, flickering shadows.

Commander Gaius Tarn, a stern figure in polished armor, oversees the room from a raised platform, his hard gaze missing nothing. His hand rests casually on the pommel of his weapon, and his stance speaks volumes about his readiness to leap into action. Four formidable Conclave Guards, bristling with weapons, stand watch around the room, their eyes alert for any signs of trouble.

Rift Shard Cage Trap

The Rift Shard is protected by a complex, mechanical cage trap designed to prevent unauthorized access. The cage is made of heavy iron bars and seems to hum with energy.

Triggering the Trap

If anyone attempts to simply reach in or force the cage open to remove the Rift Shard without first disarming the mechanism, the trap is triggered. The bars of the cage constrict around the Shard, and an electrical surge is released in a 15-foot radius. Each creature within that area must make a DC 15 Dexterity saving throw, taking 22 (4d10) lightning damage on a failed save, or half as much damage on a successful one.

Detecting the Trap

A character can spot the trap with a successful DC 18 Perception or Investigation check, revealing the various gears, pulleys, and coils hidden within the cage's design. The DC drops to 15 if the character has proficiency with Tinker's Tools, as they would be familiar with the mechanical workings.

Disarming the Trap

To disarm the trap, a character can use Thieves' Tools or Tinker's Tools to tamper with the mechanism, requiring a successful DC 18 Dexterity check. On a successful check, the trap is disarmed, and the cage can be safely opened to remove the Rift Shard.

However, if the character fails this check by 5 or more, they accidentally trigger the trap. If Commander Tarn or the Conclave Guards are not already alerted, they will be by this action.

Remember, the room is being watched by the well-trained eyes of Commander Tarn and his guards. Any attempt to tamper with the cage is likely to attract attention, so the party might need to create a diversion or find a way to work undetected.

For Characters Aligned with Iron Conclave

For characters aligned with the Iron Conclave, this is a moment of triumph. Their task is to assist Tarn in bringing the Rift Shard to the Ritual Chamber, to accomplish the Conclave's ultimate goal - the eradication of all magic. They may need to convince Tarn of their loyalty, especially if their methods have been unconventional. This could involve a social challenge, with potential persuasion or deception checks.

For Characters Aligned with Underground Resistance

For those aligned with the Underground Resistance, this encounter is the biggest challenge yet. They must somehow remove the Rift Shard from its guarded position without being overwhelmed by Tarn and his guards. Stealth or deception may be their best bet. Alternatively, they could try to create a diversion, drawing away some or all of the guards. A direct confrontation is likely to be tough, but if it comes to a fight, targeting the guards before engaging Tarn may be a good strategy.

Conclave Guards (Brute)

Remember that these are not ordinary guards. They have been chosen for this duty due to their loyalty and exceptional abilities. Feel free to increase their hit points or give them additional abilities to reflect their elite status.

Lair Actions

On initiative count 20 (losing initiative ties), Tarn can take a lair action to cause one of the following mechanical effects; he can't use the same effect two rounds in a row:

Tarn activates the fortress's defenses. Mechanical crossbows hidden in the walls pop out and fire at one target that Tarn can see. The target must make a DC 15 Dexterity saving throw, taking 22 (4d10) piercing damage on a failed save, or half as much damage on a successful one.

Tarn signals for reinforcements. Two Conclave Guards enter the room from a hidden door and join the fight.

Tarn triggers a fail-safe, causing the floor around the Rift Shard to become electrified. Each creature within 15 feet of the Shard must succeed on a DC 14 Dexterity saving throw or take 11 (2d10) lightning damage.

Monster

Conclave Guards (Brute)

NPC

Commander Gaius Tarn

Ritual Chamber

The most important room in the fortress, this is where the Iron Conclave plans to perform their magic-draining ritual.

The Ritual Chamber is a large, circular room with high ceilings and lined with cold, grey stone. The air is thick with tension and a sense of impending finality. In the center of the room, bound by shackles, is the figure of Ancient Lirael, her eyes radiating a sense of desperation and defiance. Around her, in strategic positions, stand the Conclave guards. They are grim, their faces hidden behind helmets, and their bodies adorned in the armor of their respective ranks. The Conclave Executioners, particularly, are an imposing sight. Their rune-inscribed armor shimmers eerily, and their magic-dampening weapons give off a sense of dread.

In this pivotal location of the Iron Conclave Fortress, the Ritual Chamber is heavily guarded and secured. This room serves as the final stage for the characters' mission. The room's design and aesthetic reflects the Conclave's dedication to eradicating magic.

Present in the room are Conclave Guards of two ranks: Brutes and Elites. Brutes are standard Conclave guards, well-trained and well-armed. Elites, however, are a cut above, showcasing superior battle prowess and dedication to their cause.

Most imposing of all are the Conclave Executioners. These ultimate enforcers of the Iron Conclave are dressed in heavy, rune-inscribed armor and wield massive weapons capable of dampening magic. Their identities remain shrouded in mystery, and their mere presence signifies the Conclave's intent to quash serious threats. The sight of an Executioner is enough to make even the bravest hearts quake.

The room also contains Ancient Lirael, a mentor to many in the Resistance, held captive and forced to participate in a ritual that could end all magic.

Ritual Chamber Trap

The Ritual Chamber houses a complex mechanical trap for added security. Concealed beneath the stone floor tiles, a meticulously constructed network of tension wires connect to a hidden lever at the entrance to the room. Pulling this lever activates the trap, releasing a deadly barrage of arrows from ingeniously hidden compartments within the room's walls.

Detecting the trap isn't easy and requires careful observation. The faint lines of the floor tiles, the barely noticeable gaps in the walls, and the concealed lever are the only telltale signs. Characters may attempt a Wisdom (Perception) check (DC 18) to spot these unusual features. Alternatively, if they have a suspicion of a trap and decide to look for mechanisms, they can perform an Intelligence (Investigation) check (DC 18) to discover the trap's presence.

Upon detecting the trap, disarming it presents another challenge. This can be achieved by carefully following the tension wires to the lever and delicately adjusting it to defuse the trap. A successful Dexterity (Thieves' Tools) check (DC 20) will safely disarm the trap without triggering it.

The Final Ritual

Destruction of Magic (Iron Conclave Victory)

Task: The Iron Conclave-aligned characters must convince or compel Ancient Lirael to conduct the ritual with the Rift Shard.

First, they will need to succeed in a Charisma (Persuasion) or Charisma (Intimidation) check (DC 22) to convince or coerce Ancient Lirael.

If they succeed, they then need to cast the ritual. This requires one of them to cast a spell of 5th level or higher while holding the Rift Shard. On a successful Arcana check (DC 18), the spell is absorbed by the shard and triggers the ritual, wiping out all magic in the world.

Upon the successful execution of the ritual using the Rift Shard, the Iron Conclave manages to eradicate magic. In D&D terms, this results in the following:

Spellcasting is impossible: No character, whether PC or NPC, can cast spells anymore. Any attempts to use spellcasting abilities simply fail.

Magic items lose their properties: Any item that previously had magical properties becomes a mundane version of that item. For example, a +1 Longsword would simply become a regular Longsword. Potions of healing turn into regular water, and a Wand of Magic Missiles becomes a mundane stick.

Creatures reliant on magic lose their abilities: Any creatures that use magic as a core part of their existence are affected drastically. For example, Elementals, who are formed from pure magic, might disappear completely or become weakened versions of themselves. Magical beasts might lose special abilities or resistances that were magical in nature. This can fundamentally change the balance of power in the world and result in some interesting scenarios for the DM to play with.

Preservation of Magic (Resistance Victory)

Task: The Underground Resistance-aligned characters must prevent the Iron Conclave from performing the ritual.

They need to retrieve the Rift Shard without alerting the guards. This requires a successful Dexterity (Stealth) check (DC 20) or Charisma (Deception) check (DC 20) to bluff their way past the guards.

Once they have the shard, they need to escape the fortress. This will require a successful Group Dexterity (Stealth) check (DC 18) to evade detection or a successful Charisma (Performance) check (DC 16) to create a distraction.

If the Underground Resistance prevents the ritual from happening, the status quo is maintained:

Magic continues to operate as normal: All rules regarding magic and spellcasting from the Player's Handbook and other sourcebooks continue to be valid. There are no additional checks or conditions for the use of magic.

Magic items retain their properties: Magic items continue to function as described in their respective descriptions.

Magical creatures are unaffected: All creatures with magical abilities or properties continue to exist as described in their Monster Manual entries or other sources.

Balance (Compromise)

Task: The characters must modify the ritual using the Nexus Locket to balance the magic instead of eradicating it.

They first need to secure the Nexus Locket. The location of the Locket can be a subplot, requiring its own set of tasks and checks.

Once they have the Locket, they need to infiltrate the Ritual Chamber. This requires successful Stealth, Deception, or Performance checks as mentioned earlier.

Inside the chamber, they must interfere with the ritual. This requires a character with the Locket to cast a spell of 5th level or higher while holding the Rift Shard. On a successful Arcana check (DC 22), the spell is absorbed by the shard and triggers the altered ritual, balancing magic in the world.

The Rift Shard, altered by the Nexus Locket during the ritual, balances magic. Implementing this in D&D could look like:

Magic becomes predictable: The chaos of wild magic is tamed. Any rule or event involving randomness in magic, such as Wild Magic Surges, is nullified.

Spellcasting requires focus: Whenever a spell is cast, the caster must succeed on a DC 10 Arcana check. On a failure, the spell doesn't consume a spell slot but fails to produce its effect. This reflects the new requirement for precise control in spellcasting.

Magic items operate at variable efficiency: When a magic item is used, roll a d20. On a roll of 10 or below, the item operates at its minimum efficiency (lowest possible damage, shortest duration, fewest targets, etc.). On a roll of 11 or above, the item operates at maximum efficiency (maximum damage, longest duration, most targets, etc.).

Magic Chaos (Failure)

Task: The characters fail to control the Rift Shard, triggering a second "Shattering".

This could happen if they attempt any of the tasks above but fail the crucial checks.

Alternatively, this could be a deliberate act. A character might decide to destroy the Rift Shard, unleashing its raw magical energy. This requires a Strength (Athletics) check (DC 25) to shatter the shard or an attack roll against the shard's AC (20) and HP (50). If the shard is destroyed, it triggers the second "Shattering", causing magic to become chaotic and uncontrollable.

Failure to control the Rift Shard causes a second "Shattering", resulting in chaotic magic surges:

Frequent Wild Magic Surges: Any time a spell is cast or a magic item is used, the DM can use the Random Table to trigger random events.

For Characters Aligned with Iron Conclave

Iron Conclave-aligned characters have a clear mission: drain all magic using the Rift Shard. To accomplish this, they must convince or force Lirael to cast the ritual. Roleplay might be the best approach, attempting to persuade her to their cause with a successful Charisma (Persuasion) check against Lirael's Insight (DC 18). If characters resort to deception, a successful Charisma (Deception) check (DC 20) could deceive her into thinking they share her ideals. Alternatively, they might try to intimidate her into submission with a successful Charisma (Intimidation) check (DC 22), but this approach might harden her resolve and could lead to complications. The moment of casting the ritual should be a climax full of drama.

For Characters Aligned with Underground Resistance

Resistance-aligned characters face a more complex challenge. They need to secure the Shard, free Ancient Lirael, and escape the fortress, all while ensuring the ritual is cast to balance, not eradicate, all magic. This will require the characters have the Nexus Locket. They might consider stealth, requiring a successful Group Dexterity (Stealth) check (DC 18) to approach without drawing attention. If they attempt deception, they'll need a successful Charisma (Deception) check (DC 20) to bluff their way past the guards. Characters might also consider creating a distraction outside the chamber, needing a successful Intelligence (Performance) or Charisma (Performance) check (DC 16) to draw guards away. If they decide to confront the guards head-on, be sure they're prepared for a challenging battle. Regardless of their approach, freeing Lirael will require a successful Dexterity (Sleight of Hand) check (DC 16) as well as a Dexterity check (using Thieves' Tools) DC 16 to unlock her shackles without alerting the guards.

Lair Actions

On initiative count 20 (losing initiative ties), the Conclave can take a lair action to cause one of the following effects; the Conclave can't use the same effect two rounds in a row:

The Conclave Executioners activate their magic-dampening weapons, causing a pulse that disrupts magic use. For the next round, any magic cast within the chamber has a 50% chance of failing.

The Conclave guards move with a level of coordination that showcases their rigorous training. For the next round, they have advantage on all attack rolls and saving throws.

The room's security system activates, sounding an alarm throughout the fortress. Additional Conclave Guards are alerted and will arrive in 1d4 rounds.

Monster

Conclave Guards (Brute)

Conclave Guards (Elite)

Conclave Executioners

NPC

Ancient Lirael

Resolution

As the DM, there are many ways in which the campaign can be resolved. Below are four based on how the characters are aligned with different factions in the game:

Destruction of Magic (Iron Conclave Victory)

If the characters aligned with the Iron Conclave manage to find the Rift Shard and use it to conduct the ritual in the Ritual Chamber, all magic is destroyed. The world would face a new era, one without the influence of magic. Depending on the fallout, characters might need to help with the transition, calming chaotic elements, or face the consequences of their actions as the world reacts to this dramatic shift.

Preservation of Magic (Resistance Victory)

If the characters aligned with the Resistance manage to secure the Rift Shard before the Iron Conclave, or otherwise stop the ritual, but are not able to alter the ritual with the use of the Nexus Locket, the current state of magic is preserved, but not yet secured. Still, the characters are hailed as heroes among magic users. Their next steps might involve dealing with the remnants of the Iron Conclave, recovering the Nexus

Locket and attempting to cast the balancing ritual, helping rebuild the Undercity, and figuring out how to secure the Rift Shard to ensure it doesn't fall into the wrong hands again.

Balance (Compromise)

With the help of the Nexus Locket, the characters manage to alter the Rift Shard during the ritual, causing it to instead cast a balancing ritual that stabilizes all magic. With the balance of magic restored to the world, the Resistance has truly achieved their greatest goal. However, the Iron Conclave must be dealt with, as well as the victims transformed into unstable monstrosities for the past decade who may now have their humanity abruptly restored, but still need to heal. The characters can address how to rebuild trust by working with former Iron Conclave followers and assisting those deeply scarred by magic to address their fears and adjust to the new age.

Alternatively, perhaps the characters manage to negotiate a compromise between the two factions before conducting any ritual, using the Rift Shard to alter the nature of magic in a way that addresses the Iron Conclave's concerns while preserving the essence of magic. This resolution might involve a lot of diplomacy, dealing with faction leaders and defusing potential conflicts. It may also lead to entirely new adventures as the world adjusts to the changes.

Magic Chaos (Failure)

The characters fail to control the Rift Shard and a second "Shattering" occurs with a chaotic surge of magic. This could lead to a variety of strange phenomena and new threats, potentially setting up a new adventure as the characters have to deal with the aftermath.

Random Encounters

Random Encounters

The DM can use the following table to add a random encounter at any time in the game:

1d20	Random Encounter
1	A small pack of Echo Hounds has picked up the party's scent and is tracking them.
2	A Prohibition Construct on patrol has detected the party's magical items or abilities.
3	The party stumbles upon a Shatterbeast feasting on a recent kill. It may see the party as its next meal.
4	The party encounters a group of Underground Resistance fighters hiding from Conclave Guards.
5	The party stumbles upon a seemingly harmless Nexus Wisp. However, it is territorial and defends its space with surprising bursts of magic.
6	The party encounters a distressed member of The Shattered, who is struggling to control their powers and causing magical chaos.
7	A group of Iron Wraiths is wandering in search of magic users to attack. They sense the party's presence.
8	The party finds a Rune Golem, motionless until it detects a threat to its programmed protectee.
9	A group of Conclave Guards is marching towards the party's position. They haven't seen the party yet, but they soon will.
10	The party comes across an Arcane Echo, violently re-enacting its last moments before The Shattering.
11	The party encounters an Unraveled, its physical form flickering and changing in a disconcerting display of unstable magic.
12	A Conclave Executioner, the ultimate enforcer of the Iron Conclave, is nearby. His presence indicates a serious threat is at hand.
13	The party finds a group of the Reclaimed Dead, their fragmented memories causing them to act out strange and eerie routines.
14	The party stumbles upon a pair of Shatterbeasts, locked in a territorial dispute.
15	A rogue Prohibition Construct, malfunctioning and aggressive, detects the party and attacks.
16	The party encounters a peaceful Nexus Wisp, its glow offering a temporary respite from the darkness.
17	An Arcane Echo appears before the party, its sudden violent outburst a testament to its agonizing confusion.
18	A Rune Golem, having mistaken the party for threats, moves to engage.
19	The party encounters a lost member of The Shattered, in need of help to control his volatile powers.
20	The party stumbles upon a gathering of Conclave Guards, planning an imminent strike on a nearby Underground Resistance hideout.

Scaling Monsters

Use the following table for party size to increase the number of monsters:

Party Size	Increase number by
5-8	x 1.5
9-12	x 2
13	x 2.5

Use the following table for party level to increase the number of monsters:

Party Level	Increase number by
5-8	x 1.5
9-12	x 2
13-15	x 2.5
Level 16+	x 3.5

Now take the number for the party and the level and add the two together. For instance, if you have a Party Size of 5 with an average Party Level of 10, then you would add 1.5 + 2.5 to get 4 times the monsters. 3 creatures for a level 10 party are no challenge, especially if there are 6 or 7 PC's. Increase that to 12, and suddenly you have a challenge. Feel free to adjust as you see fit.

In addition to scaling monster, many of the traps and puzzles in the game have a sliding scale that the DM can use to change the level of difficulty depending on the skillset of the characters.

Brute and Elite Creatures

Many creatures, such as Conclave Guards, can have Brute and Elite versions. These upskilled versions of the base creature can be used by DMs to make conflicts more challenging.

Monsters

Monsters

Arcane Echo

Medium undead, chaotic neutral

Armor Class: 12

Hit Points: 45 (10d8)

Speed: 0 ft., fly 30 ft. (hover)

STR	DEX	CON	INT	WIS	CHA
1 (-5)	15 (+2)	10 (+0)	12 (+1)	14 (+2)	20 (+5)

Damage Resistances: acid, fire, lightning, thunder; bludgeoning, piercing, and slashing from nonmagical attacks

Damage Immunities: cold, necrotic, poison

Condition Immunities: charmed, exhaustion, grappled, paralyzed, petrified, poisoned, prone, restrained

Senses: darkvision 60 ft., passive Perception 12

Languages: the languages it knew in life

Challenge: 4 (1,100 XP)

Incorporeal Movement: The Arcane Echo can move through other creatures and objects as if they were difficult terrain. It takes 5 (1d10) force damage if it ends its turn inside an object.

Magic Resistance: The Arcane Echo has advantage on saving throws against spells and other magical effects.

Actions

Unstable Magic (Recharge 5-6): The Arcane Echo releases a burst of unstable magical energy. Each creature within 15 feet of it must make a DC 15 Dexterity saving throw, taking 18 (4d8) force damage on a failed save, or half as much damage on a successful one. The Arcane Echo can choose to make the energy fire, cold, lightning, or necrotic instead of force, changing the damage type to match.

Arcane Touch: Melee Spell Attack: +7 to hit, reach 5 ft., one target. Hit: 14 (4d6) force damage.

Arcane Echoes can pose a significant threat to parties that aren't prepared for their damage output, but their low AC and hit points make them relatively easy to deal with if they can be targeted and focused down. They could be used to great effect in encounters that feature other, more robust threats that keep the party occupied.

Arcane Echoes are spectral remnants of those consumed by the cataclysm of The Shattering. They appear as ethereal, semi-transparent figures, seemingly frozen in the exact moment of their tragic end. Though their exact appearance varies, they always bear the look of a magical practitioner caught in a moment of intense casting, hands outstretched, eyes wide, mouth open as though caught in a silent scream or a word of power.

Their bodies seem to be made of pure magical energy, flickering and wavering like a candle flame caught in a breeze. This energy pulses with an eerie light, usually mirroring the color of their magic in life. The stronger the echo, the brighter and more defined the figure.

Their ethereal form often trails off into wisps of energy, as though they're slowly disintegrating or being blown away by a wind only they can feel. These wisps can form ghostly approximations of the robes or clothing they wore in life.

A closer look at their faces might reveal a haunting glimpse into their final moments—eyes filled with surprise, fear, determination, or sorrow. Yet, despite their tragic state, Arcane Echoes are also a poignant reminder of the power and potential magic once held in this world.

Conclave Guard

Medium humanoid (human), lawful neutral

Armor Class: 17 (splint)

Hit Points: 52 (8d8 + 16)

Speed: 30 ft.

STR	DEX	CON	INT	WIS	CHA
16 (+3)	12 (+1)	14 (+2)	10 (+0)	11 (+0)	10 (+0)

Skills: Perception +2

Senses: passive Perception 12

Languages: Common

Challenge: 2 (450 XP)

Actions

Multiattack: The Conclave Guard makes two melee attacks or two ranged attacks.

Longsword: Melee Weapon Attack: +5 to hit, reach 5 ft., one target. Hit: 7 (1d8 + 3) slashing damage, or 8 (1d10 + 3) slashing damage if used with two hands.

Heavy Crossbow: Ranged Weapon Attack: +3 to hit, range 100/400 ft., one target. Hit: 6 (1d10 + 1) piercing damage.

Reactions

Parry: The guard adds 2 to its AC against one melee attack that would hit it. To do so, the guard must see the attacker and be wielding a melee weapon.

Iron Conclave's Training (3/day): Whenever the guard makes a saving throw against a spell or other magical effect, they can add a d4 to the roll, representing the specialized training they have received to resist magic.

Conclave Guards are imposing figures, standing tall and muscular, often over six feet in height. They are dressed in uniform, dark iron chain mail that covers them from neck to feet, leaving no part unprotected. The chain mail glimmers subtly under any light source, signifying the enchantments that have been woven into the very fabric of their armor.

Over their chain mail, they wear tabards of a deep crimson hue, the color of fresh blood, emblazoned with the emblem of the Iron Conclave – a stylized, silver, wrought iron gate. This insignia signifies their loyalty and allegiance to their cause.

Their helmets are full-faced, forged from the same dark iron as their chain mail. The only visible part of their face is their eyes, glowing with a steely resolve, often reflecting the hard, no-nonsense demeanor that they carry with them.

In their hands, they grip massive halberds, the blades of which are designed to resemble the same iron gate symbol, an aesthetic choice that ties in their weapon with their role as protectors of the Conclave's will. The shaft of the halberd is as black as obsidian and inlaid with runic symbols that glow faintly, a testament to the magical enhancements that aid them in their duty.

Overall, their presence is one of calculated authority and formidable power, a visual representation of the iron will of the Conclave they serve. They stand as unwavering sentinels, embodiments of the Iron Conclave's determination to eradicate magic from the world.

The Conclave Guards are disciplined soldiers who have sworn loyalty to the Iron Conclave and its mission of suppressing magic. Trained to fight against spellcasters, they have a special understanding of how to resist magic and use that knowledge to their advantage in combat. They are stern, dedicated, and unyielding, believing that their cause is just and necessary for the protection of the realm. While not necessarily villains, they are formidable adversaries for those who oppose the Conclave's goals.

Conclave Guard (Brute)

Medium humanoid (human), lawful neutral

Armor Class: 16 (Chain Mail, Shield)

Hit Points: 75 (10d8 + 30)

Speed: 30 ft.

STR	DEX	CON	INT	WIS	CHA
18 (+4)	12 (+1)	16 (+3)	10 (+0)	12 (+1)	10 (+0)

Skills: Athletics +7, Perception +4

Senses: passive Perception 14

Languages: Common

Challenge: 5 (1,800 XP)

Brute Force. Melee weapon attacks deal one extra die of damage when the brute hits.

Actions

Multiattack: The Conclave Guard (Brute) makes two melee attacks.

Longsword: Melee Weapon Attack: +7 to hit, reach 5 ft., one target. Hit: 15 (2d10 + 4) slashing damage, or 11 (2d8 + 4) slashing damage if used with one hand.

Spear: Melee or Ranged Weapon Attack: +7 to hit, reach 5 ft. or range 20/60 ft., one target. Hit: 13 (2d8 + 4) piercing damage, or 14 (2d10 + 4) piercing damage if used with two hands to make a melee attack.

Conclave Guard (Elite)

Medium humanoid (human), lawful neutral

Armor Class: 18 (Plate Mail)

Hit Points: 105 (14d8 + 14)

Speed: 30 ft.

STR	DEX	CON	INT	WIS	CHA
16 (+3)	12 (+1)	12 (+1)	14 (+2)	14 (+2)	14 (+2)

Saving Throws: Str +6, Con +4

Skills: Athletics +6, Perception +5

Senses: passive Perception 15

Languages: Common

Challenge: 5 (1,800 XP)

Parry. The elite adds 2 to its AC against one melee attack that would hit it. To do so, the elite must see the attacker and be wielding a melee weapon.

Actions

Multiattack. The Conclave Guard (Elite) makes two melee attacks.

Longsword. Melee Weapon Attack: +6 to hit, reach 5 ft., one target. Hit: 8 (1d10 + 3) slashing damage, or 7 (1d8 + 3) slashing damage if used with one hand.

Heavy Crossbow. Ranged Weapon Attack: +4 to hit, range 100/400 ft., one target. Hit: 6 (1d10 + 1) piercing damage.

These guards represent a significant increase in threat over the basic Conclave Guard, with the brute focusing more on raw physical power and the elite offering more tactical and versatile combat options.

Conclave Executioner

Medium humanoid (human), lawful evil

Armor Class: 18 (plate, shield)

Hit Points: 120 (16d8 + 48)

Speed: 30 ft.

STR	DEX	CON	INT	WIS	CHA
20 (+5)	12 (+1)	16 (+3)	14 (+2)	14 (+2)	12 (+1)

Saving Throws: Str +9, Con +7

Skills: Intimidation +5, Athletics +9

Damage Resistances: bludgeoning, piercing, and slashing from nonmagical attacks not made with adamantine weapons

Condition Immunities: charmed, frightened

Senses: passive Perception 12

Languages: Common

Challenge: 9 (5,000 XP)

Magic Resistance: The Conclave Executioner has advantage on saving throws against spells and other magical effects.

Magic Weapons: The Conclave Executioner's weapon attacks are magical.

Rune Inscribed Armor: Any spell of 5th level or lower cast from outside the armor has no effect on the Conclave Executioner nor can it pass through the armor. The spell simply dissipates upon contact with the armor.

Actions

Multiattack: The Conclave Executioner makes two attacks with its greataxe.

Greataxe: Melee Weapon Attack: +9 to hit, reach 5 ft., one target. Hit: 17 (1d12 + 5) slashing damage plus 9 (2d8) force damage.

Dampening Wave (Recharge 5–6): The Conclave Executioner slams its weapon into the ground, creating a wave of anti-magic force. Each creature within 20 feet of the executioner must make a DC 16 Constitution saving throw. On a failed save, the creature can't cast spells until the end of its next turn.

Conclave Executioners are the ultimate enforcers of the Iron Conclave, sent to quash serious threats to the Conclave's authority. Their rune-inscribed armor protects them from magic, and their magic-dampening weapons help them control enemy spellcasters.

Conclave Executioners are imposing figures who carry an aura of dread with them wherever they go. They stand tall, often reaching over 6 feet in height, and are always heavily armored. The armor is a bleak matte black, adorned with dull silver runes that are the signature of the Iron Conclave. These runes are anti-magical, flickering with a cold, silvery light when magic is nearby.

The helmets they wear are completely devoid of any facial features, presenting an impassive and terrifying visage. The only distinguishing feature is a narrow horizontal slit that glows with an ominous red light, allowing them to see but revealing nothing of what lies inside. It gives the Executioner a robotic, inhuman feel, furthering the sense of dread they inspire.

Executioners carry massive weapons, often greatswords or halberds, etched with the same silvery runes as their armor. The size and design of these weapons are purposefully intimidating, serving as a stark reminder of the power the Iron Conclave wields. Despite the weight, Executioners wield these weapons with surprising agility and deadly precision.

Their presence is always accompanied by a palpable pressure, a heaviness in the air that signifies their dedication to their singular, grim task. To see a Conclave Executioner is to come face-to-face with the relentless pursuit of magic's eradication.

Echo Hound

Medium monstrosity, unaligned

Armor Class: 13

Hit Points: 45 (6d8 + 18)

Speed: 40 ft.

STR	DEX	CON	INT	WIS	CHA
14 (+2)	16 (+3)	16 (+3)	3 (-4)	12 (+1)	6 (-2)

Skills: Perception +3, Stealth +5

perceived through the distortion they create in the air and the high-pitched, echoing sounds they emit.

When they move, they displace air and sound around them, creating visible ripples, like heatwaves on a hot day, warping the view of whatever lies behind them. These distortions, along with the faint shimmering outline of their forms, are the only physical presence that betrays their existence. Their forms, when vaguely visible, bear a resemblance to hounds but with elongated bodies and unnaturally twisted, almost spectral limbs that seem to flicker in and out of the physical plane.

Their echo-like sounds range from high-frequency whines to deep, resonant growls that seem to come from everywhere and nowhere at once. When they "bark" or "howl," the sounds bounce off surfaces, creating a disorienting sonic landscape that makes pinpointing their exact location nearly impossible.

When they attack, the only warning is a sudden intensification of their high-pitched sound, followed by the painful sensation of their ethereal jaws clamping down. To the Echo Hounds' prey, it can often feel like they are being attacked by the very sound waves the creatures emit.

Iron Wraith

Medium undead, lawful evil

Armor Class: 18 (ethereal armor)

Hit Points: 110 (20d8 + 20)

Speed: 0 ft., fly 30 ft. (hover)

STR	DEX	CON	INT	WIS	CHA
16 (+3)	14 (+2)	12 (+1)	10 (+0)	12 (+1)	16 (+3)

Saving Throws: Wis +4, Cha +6

Damage Resistances: acid, fire, lightning, thunder; bludgeoning, piercing, and slashing from nonmagical attacks

Damage Immunities: cold, necrotic, poison; bludgeoning, piercing, and slashing from magical attacks

Condition Immunities: charmed, exhaustion, frightened, grappled, paralyzed, petrified, poisoned, prone, restrained

Senses: darkvision 60 ft., passive Perception 11

Languages: the languages it knew in life

Challenge: 10 (5,900 XP)

Incorporeal Movement: The Iron Wraith can move through other creatures and objects as if they were difficult terrain. It takes 5 (1d10) force damage if it ends its turn inside an object.

Damage Immunities: thunder

Condition Immunities: deafened

Senses: blindsight 60 ft. (blind beyond this radius), passive Perception 13

Languages: —

Challenge: 4 (1,100 XP)

Keen Hearing: The Echo Hound has advantage on Wisdom (Perception) checks that rely on hearing.

Invisibility: The Echo Hound is invisible.

Sound Travel: The Echo Hound can teleport up to 40 feet to an unoccupied space it can hear but has not seen.

Actions

Multiattack: The Echo Hound makes two bite attacks.

Bite: Melee Weapon Attack: +5 to hit, reach 5 ft., one target. Hit: 7 (1d8 + 3) piercing damage.

Sonic Screech (Recharge 5–6): The Echo Hound unleashes a devastating screech. Each creature within 20 feet of the Echo Hound must make a DC 13 Constitution saving throw. On a failed save, a creature takes 10 (3d6) thunder damage and is stunned until the end of its next turn. On a successful save, the creature takes half as much damage and isn't stunned.

Echo Hounds hunt in packs and are incredibly challenging to fight due to their invisibility and ability to move through sound. Their Sonic Screech ability can paralyze multiple opponents at once, making them deadly predators.

Echo Hounds are surreal, unsettling creatures to behold, primarily because they're never truly seen but rather

Magic Resistance: The Iron Wraith has advantage on saving throws against spells and other magical effects.

Antimagic Susceptibility: The Iron Wraith is incapacitated while in the area of an antimagic field. If targeted by dispel magic, the Iron Wraith must succeed on a Constitution saving throw against the caster's spell save DC or fall unconscious for 1 minute.

Turn Immunity: The Iron Wraith is immune to effects that turn undead.

Actions

Multiattack: The Iron Wraith makes two longsword attacks.

Ethereal Longsword: Melee Weapon Attack: +6 to hit, reach 5 ft., one target. Hit: 8 (1d10 + 3) slashing damage. If the target is a creature, it must succeed on a DC 16 Wisdom saving throw or become frightened of the Iron Wraith for 1 minute. The frightened target can repeat the saving throw at the end of each of its turns, with disadvantage if the Iron Wraith is within line of sight, ending the effect on itself on a success.

Antimagic Burst (Recharge 5-6): The Iron Wraith releases a burst of anti-magical energy. Each creature and magical object within 10 feet of it must make a DC 16 Constitution saving throw. On a failure, a creature takes 18 (4d8) force damage and can't cast spells or use magical abilities until the end of its next turn. Magical objects are suppressed until the end of the Iron Wraith's next turn. On a success, a creature takes half the damage and isn't otherwise affected.

The Iron Wraith is a formidable enemy, especially for magic-focused parties. Its ability to pass through physical barriers, coupled with its anti-magic capabilities, make it a unique and challenging opponent. Its Turn Immunity also prevents it from being easily banished or controlled by clerics or paladins.

Iron Wraiths are spectral beings that exude an eerie, otherworldly presence. Standing roughly seven feet tall, they are taller than most humans, their size made even more imposing by their spectral nature. The Iron Conclave controls these creatures with Conclave Clerics, an elite group who have special permission and rules to use magic.

Their semi-transparent bodies take on the appearance of heavily armored knights, the form shrouded in a soft, silvery glow that is oddly soothing and terrifying at the same time. The armor they wear seems to be a part of them, bearing intricate engravings and anti-magic symbols that flicker with a dull, cold light.

Their helmets completely obscure their faces, leaving only two glowing pinpoints where eyes should be. These points of light give off an intense, penetrating gaze that seems to look right through whoever they focus on.

In their hands, they wield weapons made from a similar spectral material as their bodies. These weapons are massive, each one designed to instill fear and capable of swiping through magical defenses as if they were mere illusions.

When an Iron Wraith moves, it is a mix of fluidity and rigidity, as if they were once a creature of flesh and bone now bound to an ethereal form. Each step leaves a brief, shimmering afterimage in the air that quickly fades, and their passage is eerily silent, the only sound being the faint echoes of ghostly chains.

Nexus Wisp

Tiny elemental, neutral

Armor Class: 13

Hit Points: 18 (4d4 + 8)

Speed: 0 ft., fly 40 ft. (hover)

STR	DEX	CON	INT	WIS	CHA
3 (-4)	17 (+3)	14 (+2)	6 (-2)	11 (+0)	10 (+0)

Skills: Stealth +5

Damage Resistances: bludgeoning, piercing, and slashing from nonmagical attacks

Damage Immunities: poison

Condition Immunities: exhaustion, grappled, paralyzed, petrified, poisoned, prone, restrained, unconscious

Senses: darkvision 60 ft., passive Perception 10

Languages: understands the languages of its creator but can't speak

Challenge: 1/2 (100 XP)

Invisibility: The wisp can turn invisible until it attacks or until its concentration ends (as if concentrating on a spell).

Magic Resistance: The wisp has advantage on saving throws against spells and other magical effects.

Actions

Shock: Melee Spell Attack: +5 to hit, reach 5 ft., one creature. Hit: 9 (2d6 + 2) lightning damage.

Ethereal Burst (Recharge 6): The wisp gathers all its energy and releases it in a burst of magic. Each creature within 10 feet of the wisp must make a DC 13 Dexterity saving throw, taking 14 (4d6) force damage on a failed save, or half as much damage on a successful one.

Nexus Wisps can be a surprise for adventurers who underestimate them due to their size. Their ability to turn invisible and their Ethereal Burst make them a threat to be taken seriously, especially in groups.

Nexus Wisps are tiny, ethereal creatures that seem to be made entirely of concentrated, pulsating magical energy. They are radiant entities, about the size of a small bird, emanating a soft, enchanting light that shifts through a rainbow of colors, giving them an otherworldly, captivating presence.

Their shape is amorphous and fluid, often resembling a small cloud or cluster of starlight, with shimmering tendrils of energy constantly dancing around their core. These tendrils move in response to their emotions and curiosity, flaring out or curling inward as if alive themselves.

The most striking feature of a Nexus Wisp, however, is its "eye" - a bright, single point of concentrated light within their core that they use to observe their surroundings. This eye is incredibly expressive and is capable of conveying a range of emotions, from curiosity to fear, despite the wisp's lack of any other discernible facial features.

When a Nexus Wisp moves, it does so by floating gently through the air, leaving a short-lived trail of sparkling light behind it. They move with an airy grace and a seeming curiosity about the world, fluttering around and through objects in their path as they explore their surroundings.

Prohibition Construct

Large construct, unaligned

Armor Class: 17 (natural armor)

Hit Points: 114 (12d10 + 48)

Speed: 30 ft.

STR	DEX	CON	INT	WIS	CHA
20 (+5)	9 (-1)	18 (+4)	6 (-2)	12 (+1)	5 (-3)

Damage Immunities: poison, psychic; bludgeoning, piercing, and slashing from nonmagical attacks not made with adamantine weapons

Condition Immunities: charmed, exhaustion, frightened, paralyzed, petrified, poisoned

Senses: darkvision 120 ft., passive Perception 11

Languages: understands the languages of its creator but can't speak

Challenge: 8 (3,900 XP)

Magic Resistance: The construct has advantage on saving throws against spells and other magical effects.

Antimagic Field: The construct emits an antimagic field in a 10-foot radius. The field is always active.

Actions

Multiattack: The construct makes two slam attacks.

Slam: Melee Weapon Attack: +9 to hit, reach 5 ft., one target. Hit: 14 (2d8 + 5) bludgeoning damage.

Spell Breaker (Recharge 5-6): The construct focuses the energy of its magic core and unleashes it in a blast of disruptive energy. Each creature within 30 feet of the construct must make a DC 16 Constitution saving throw. On a failed save, a creature takes 18 (4d8) force damage and can't cast spells until the end of its next turn. On a successful save, a creature takes half as much damage and isn't otherwise affected.

These constructs are designed to be a significant threat, especially to magic-users. Their constant antimagic field and ability to disrupt spellcasting make them a serious problem for any party relying heavily on magic. A clever group of adventurers might find ways to disable or avoid these constructs, or even to turn their abilities to their own advantage.

Prohibition Constructs are towering figures of intimidating design. They stand approximately 10 feet tall, resembling humanoid knights, but where one would expect to see human features, the Constructs instead present an unsettling blend of mechanical and arcane aesthetics.

Their bodies are comprised of sleek, dark metal plates intricately carved with a network of glowing runic symbols. These runes pulse with a muted blue light, indicating the controlled magical core within. The Constructs' heads are faceless, save for a single, radiant glyph that shines from where one would expect eyes to be. This glyph scans their surroundings, flickering and intensifying whenever it detects the presence of magic.

Despite their imposing size, the Prohibition Constructs move with an eerie silence and a measured grace that belies their bulk. Each movement is precise and efficient, a testament to the advanced magical and mechanical engineering behind their creation.

They are armed with massive, rune-inscribed halberds, the haft made of the same dark metal as their bodies, and the blade glowing with the same muted light as their runes. These weapons serve as both a means of attack and a symbol of their duty: to detect and suppress any use of magic.

The sight of a Prohibition Construct on patrol is a chilling reminder of the Iron Conclave's control, their formidable presence alone enough to deter most from even thinking of using magic.

Reclaimed Dead

Medium undead, chaotic neutral

Armor Class: 12

Hit Points: 67 (9d8 + 27)

Speed: 30 ft.

STR	DEX	CON	INT	WIS	CHA
16 (+3)	14 (+2)	16 (+3)	6 (-2)	10 (+0)	5 (-3)

Damage Resistances: necrotic; bludgeoning, piercing, and slashing from nonmagical attacks

Damage Immunities: poison

Condition Immunities: charmed, exhaustion, poisoned

Senses: darkvision 60 ft., passive Perception 10

Languages understands the languages it knew in life but can't speak

Challenge: 4 (1,100 XP)

Magic Resistance: The Reclaimed Dead has advantage on saving throws against spells and other magical effects.

Memory Echo: When the Reclaimed Dead is first damaged in combat, it flashes back to a moment from its past life, taking on characteristics of its former self. Roll a d6 and consult the Memory Echo table for the effect.

Actions

Multiattack: The Reclaimed Dead makes two slam attacks.

Slam: Melee Weapon Attack: +5 to hit, reach 5 ft., one target. Hit: 7 (1d8 + 3) bludgeoning damage.

Memory Echo Table

- Warrior. The Reclaimed Dead gains a multiattack with a longsword and a shield bash. It can make one attack with each.
- Mage. The Reclaimed Dead casts a random spell from its past life (DM's choice).
- Thief. The Reclaimed Dead disengages and tries to hide, using the surroundings to its advantage.
- Priest. The Reclaimed Dead uses healing magic to recover some hit points.
- Craftsman. The Reclaimed Dead fixates on a random object, trying to repair or improve it, ignoring combat until attacked again.
- Normal Life. The Reclaimed Dead stands confused, taking no action on its next turn.

This creature offers a unique twist on the typical undead enemy. The Memory Echo ability can add an unexpected twist to combat, forcing the party to quickly adapt their tactics. The fragment of humanity left in these beings could also create interesting roleplay situations or moral dilemmas.

The Reclaimed Dead are a haunting vision of life interrupted and contorted by uncontrolled magic. Unlike typical undead, their appearance is less a rotting corpse and more a spectral mirage of their former selves, infused with wild magic that glimmers beneath their semi-translucent skin.

Their bodies, once human, are now marred by magic. Parts of them may appear ethereal or partially faded, as though struggling between the realms of life and death. Other sections of their bodies may show vivid magical scarring, where wild magic has reshaped their flesh into otherworldly patterns and textures, all glowing with a faint iridescent sheen. A Priest using healing magic to recover some hit points would be unwittingly damaging itself.

Their eyes glow with an unnerving light, filled with the chaotic magic that animates them, but also the lingering traces of their past lives. These eyes often betray a sense of confusion or sorrow, providing a chilling reminder of their tragic origins.

Often, the Reclaimed Dead are found repeating fragments of their past routines in a haunting mockery of their former lives. This could manifest in a Reclaimed Dead laborer eternally attempting to complete a day's work, or a Reclaimed Dead noble eternally preparing for a never-to-happen feast.

To witness the Reclaimed Dead is to be reminded of the disastrous consequences of uncontrolled magic, adding a layer of tragedy to their frightening visage.

Rune Golem

Large construct, unaligned

Armor Class: 17 (natural armor)

Hit Points: 133 (14d10 + 56)

Speed: 30 ft.

STR	DEX	CON	INT	WIS	CHA
20 (+5)	9 (-1)	18 (+4)	3 (-4)	11 (+0)	1 (-5)

Damage Resistances: bludgeoning, piercing, and slashing from nonmagical attacks not made with adamantine weapons

Damage Immunities: poison, psychic

Condition Immunities: charmed, exhaustion, frightened, paralyzed, petrified, poisoned

Senses: darkvision 120 ft., passive Perception 10

Languages: understands the languages of its creator but can't speak

Challenge: 9 (5,000 XP)

Immutable Form: The Rune Golem is immune to any spell or effect that would alter its form.

Magic Resistance: The Rune Golem has advantage on saving throws against spells and other magical effects.

Magic Weapons: The Rune Golem's weapon attacks are magical.

Actions

Multiattack: The Rune Golem makes two melee attacks.

Slam: Melee Weapon Attack: +9 to hit, reach 5 ft., one target. Hit: 19 (3d8 + 5) bludgeoning damage.

Reshape Body (Recharge 5-6): The Rune Golem transforms parts of its body into weapons, giving its slam attacks an extra 2d8 slashing damage, or it can transform its body into a hardened shell, increasing its AC by 2. The effects last until the start of the Rune Golem's next turn.

Runic Pulse (1/day): The Rune Golem emits a burst of runic energy. Each creature within 10 feet of it must make a DC 16 Constitution saving throw, taking 21 (6d6) force damage on a failed save, or half as much damage on a successful one.

The Rune Golem is a formidable opponent, capable of dealing high damage and taking quite a few hits. It is best used in encounters where it can utilize its abilities to the fullest, such as protecting an important location or person.

Rune Golems are impressive constructs of magic and stone, standing between eight to ten feet tall. Their bodies are composed of large, irregular chunks of stone that float together in a humanoid shape, held in place by a shimmering magical aura. They are ancient artifacts of an unknown group of magic users. Their ancient origin and tough construction made them immune to the effects of The Shattering.

Each piece of stone is carved with intricate glowing runes that emit a soft, pulsating light, suggesting a vast and complex internal magic network. The light from these runes often filters out from the gaps between the stones, bathing the golem in a steady, luminescent glow.

Rune Golems lack facial features in the

traditional sense. Instead, a series of glowing runes on what would be their head provide the focal point, giving the impression of eyes and a mouth. The intensity of this glow changes as the golem "expresses" itself.

Their arms are massive and can reshape into various forms as needed. A golem might form a giant stone fist for combat, reshape its arm into a flat surface to act as a barrier, or even sprout smaller appendages to handle delicate tasks.

Despite their rocky composition, Rune Golems move with surprising grace. Their stone parts float and reposition smoothly, giving the golem a sense of fluid motion that contradicts their solid appearance. When standing still, they can appear almost like a piece of natural, albeit highly unusual, rock formation.

Shatterbeast

Large monstrosity, chaotic neutral

Armor Class: 16 (natural armor)

Hit Points: 126 (11d10 + 66)

Speed: 40 ft.

STR	DEX	CON	INT	WIS	CHA
20 (+5)	14 (+2)	22 (+6)	6 (-2)	12 (+1)	8 (-1)

Saving Throws: Dex +5, Con +9

Skills: Perception +4

Damage Resistances: bludgeoning, piercing, and slashing from nonmagical attacks

Damage Immunities: poison

Condition Immunities: poisoned

Senses: darkvision 60 ft., passive Perception 14

Languages: understands Common but can't speak

Challenge: 8 (3,900 XP)

Magic Resistance. The Shatterbeast has advantage on saving throws against spells and other magical effects.

Shattering Roar (Recharge 5-6): The Shatterbeast lets out a devastating roar infused with unstable magic. Each creature within 20 feet of the Shatterbeast must make a DC 16 Dexterity saving throw, taking 28 (8d6) force damage on a failed save, or half as much damage on a successful one.

Innate Spellcasting: The Shatterbeast's innate spellcasting ability is Wisdom (spell save DC 12). It can innately cast the following spells, requiring no material components:

- At will: magic missile (as a 1st-level spell)
- 3/day: blink

Actions

Multiattack: The Shatterbeast makes two attacks: one with its bite and one with its claws.

Bite: Melee Weapon Attack: +8 to hit, reach 5 ft., one target. Hit: 17 (2d12 + 5) piercing damage.

Claws: Melee Weapon Attack: +8 to hit, reach 5 ft., one target. Hit: 14 (2d8 + 5) slashing damage.

The Shatterbeast represents a creature transformed by the chaotic magic of the Shattering. Its innate spellcasting and Shattering Roar reflect this instability, while its physical attacks and high health showcase its monstrous, beastly nature. This creature could provide a challenging encounter for a party of adventurers.

A Shatterbeast is a terrifying sight to behold. It embodies the very essence of chaotic, unfettered magic – a creature warped by The Shattering into a monstrous form beyond recognition.

Each Shatterbeast is unique in appearance, but they all share common, horrifying features. Their bodies are a grotesque fusion of animal, humanoid, and sometimes even plant elements. A Shatterbeast might have the twisted body of a bear, but with multiple mismatched limbs, a snarling human face, and tendrils of ivy growing from its back.

Their skin is adorned with glowing arcane symbols, pulsing with magic. These symbols are not tattoos, but rather are part of the creature itself, marking where magic has seeped into its very being. They glow more intensely when the Shatterbeast uses its magical abilities, casting eerie lights in the dark.

Shatterbeasts' eyes glow with the same unstable magic that shapes their form, radiating a pure, unsettling energy. Often they have more than two eyes, some of which might be located in unorthodox places like on their limbs or torsos.

When a Shatterbeast roars, it's as if reality itself shudders. The sounds they make are unnatural, a symphony of beastly growls and otherworldly echoes, underlined by a low humming that resonates with magical energy. It's a grim reminder of the wild and unpredictable nature of magic after The Shattering.

The Shattered

Medium humanoid (any race), chaotic neutral

Armor Class: 13 (natural armor)

Hit Points: 58 (9d8 + 18)

Speed: 30 ft.

STR	DEX	CON	INT	WIS	CHA
10 (+0)	14 (+2)	14 (+2)	8 (-1)	12 (+1)	18 (+4)

Unstable Blast: Ranged Spell Attack: +7 to hit, range 150 ft., one target. Hit: 10 (3d6) force damage.

The Shattered are unpredictable and can turn the tide of battle in an instant with their erratic magic. They can be used to introduce an element of chaos into your encounters, making each fight unique and challenging.

The Shattered are among the most heartbreaking sights in the new world, symbolizing the human toll of The Shattering. They were once ordinary humans, but exposure to the raw magical energy of The Shattering has warped their minds and bodies almost beyond recognition.

Their physical appearance varies greatly, but common features include skin that's unnaturally pale or discolored, often crisscrossed with pulsing, bright blue veins that glow with unstable magic. Their eyes might glow with the same luminescence, radiating both pain and power.

Parts of their bodies may be distorted or exaggerated in impossible ways – a hand with too many fingers, a foot that has melded with the floor, or an arm that constantly shifts and changes shape. The magic within them doesn't just warp their form; it also grants them erratic magical abilities that are often beyond their control.

Around a Shattered, the air seems to vibrate with energy, sometimes causing the immediate surroundings to warp or distort. For example, objects might float slightly off the ground or twist into surreal shapes.

Their expressions are often one of deep confusion and fear, a reflection of their psychological torment. But in moments of anger or distress, their faces can contort in disturbing ways, becoming terrifying masks of raw magical fury. Their voices, too, are often distorted, reverberating with echoes or fluctuating wildly in pitch and volume. It's a sobering reminder of the devastating effects of The Shattering on the people it touched directly.

Saving Throws: Wis +4, Cha +7

Skills: Arcana +2

Damage Resistances: damage from spells; bludgeoning, piercing, and slashing from nonmagical attacks

Condition Immunities: charmed, frightened

Senses: passive Perception 11

Languages: any one language (usually Common)

Challenge: 5 (1,800 XP)

Magic Resistance: The Shattered has advantage on saving throws against spells and other magical effects.

Spellcasting: The Shattered is a 7th-level spellcaster. Its spellcasting ability is Charisma (spell save DC 15, +7 to hit with spell attacks). The Shattered can cast the following spells:

- Cantrips (at will): fire bolt, light, mage hand, prestidigitation
- 1st level (4 slots): burning hands, magic missile
- 2nd level (3 slots): scorching ray, misty step
- 3rd level (3 slots): fireball, fly
- 4th level (1 slot): confusion

Unstable Magic: When the Shattered casts a spell, roll a d20. On a 1, an unpredictable magical effect occurs. Roll on the Wild Magic Surge table (PHB p.104) to determine the result.

Actions

Multiattack: The Shattered makes two Unstable Blast attacks.

The Unraveled

Medium aberration, chaotic neutral

Armor Class: 15

Hit Points: 66 (12d8 + 12)

Speed: 30 ft.

STR	DEX	CON	INT	WIS	CHA
10 (+0)	14 (+2)	13 (+1)	18 (+4)	12 (+1)	16 (+3)

Saving Throws: Int +7, Wis +4, Cha +6

Skills: Arcana +7

Damage Immunities: poison

Condition Immunities: poisoned

Senses: darkvision 60 ft., passive Perception 11

Languages: Common, Undercommon

Challenge: 7 (2,900 XP)

Spellcasting: The Unraveled is a 10th-level spellcaster. Its spellcasting ability is Intelligence (spell save DC 15, +7 to hit with spell attacks). The Unraveled has the following wizard spells prepared:

- Cantrips (at will): mage hand, minor illusion, ray of frost
- 1st level (4 slots): magic missile, shield, witch bolt
- 2nd level (3 slots): blur, misty step
- 3rd level (3 slots): counterspell, dispel magic
- 4th level (3 slots): dimension door
- 5th level (2 slots): telekinesis

Phase Shift: The Unraveled can move through other creatures and objects as if they were difficult terrain. It takes 5 (1d10) force damage if it ends its turn inside an object.

Actions

Multiattack: The Unraveled makes two phase touch attacks.

Phase Touch: Melee Spell Attack: +7 to hit, reach 5 ft., one target. Hit: 10 (3d6) force damage.

Reactions

Unravel Reality: When the Unraveled is targeted by an attack or spell, it can use its reaction to become ethereal until the start of its next turn. The attack or spell misses, and the Unraveled can move through physical objects until its next turn. Once it uses this feature, it can't use it again until it finishes a short or long rest.

The Unraveled, with its unpredictability and powerful magic abilities, can be a challenging opponent. Its Phase Shift ability allows it to pass through physical barriers, making it hard to contain or block, while its Unravel Reality reaction makes it especially difficult to hit with targeted attacks or spells.

The Unraveled are a haunting sight to behold. They were once wizards, sorcerers, or other practitioners of the arcane, but constant exposure to the volatile magic of the post-Shattering world has altered them beyond recognition. Their bodies are stuck in a perpetual state of flux, existing in a sort of magical limbo between the physical world and the arcane realm.

Visually, an Unraveled appears almost ethereal, as if only partially existing in reality. They might phase in and out of solidity, portions of their body flickering between solid flesh, a wispy ethereal state, or even becoming briefly transparent. Their shape constantly shifts and mutates; an arm might elongate and split into multiple tendrils, only to reform into a single, solid limb moments later.

Their features are often distorted or blurred, making it hard to discern their original form. At times, their face might be recognizable as human, filled with sadness or desperation. But in the next moment, it could become a swirling vortex of color and light, an incomprehensible whirl of morphing shapes and arcane symbols.

Their clothes, if they wear any, often appear to be a part of them, merging and separating from their form in a continuous dance of transformation. Surrounding them is a subtle shimmering aura of magic, similar to heat distortion, which makes the air around them seem warped and fluid.

Their movements are unpredictable and erratic, not bound by the normal laws of physics. They might float off the ground, suddenly blink from one place to another, or stretch and distort their bodies in ways that should be impossible.

While they are dangerous and unpredictable, there's also a sense of tragedy about them – they are beings that have lost their humanity to the very power they once commanded. It has been more than a decade since The Shattering and many of The Unraveled have gone mad.

Magic Items

Magic Items

Riftblade

Type: Weapon (Longsword)

Description: This longsword appears to be made of an otherworldly, shimmering metal. It has a hollow pommel which contains a tiny rift in reality.

Properties: You have a +1 bonus to attack and damage rolls with this magic weapon. On a hit, the riftblade does an extra 1d4 force damage.

Attunement: Yes

Cloak of the Wandering Woods

Type: Wondrous item (cloak)

Description: This cloak is made from leaves and other natural materials from the Wandering Woods.

Properties: While you wear this cloak, you can use an action to become invisible, blending perfectly into natural environments. This effect lasts until you move or take an action or a reaction.

Attunement: Yes

Nexus Locket

Type: Wondrous item (amulet)

Description: A small amulet containing a tiny magical nexus.

Properties: While wearing the locket, you can use an action to restore a spent spell slot of 3rd level or lower. Once used, it can't be used again until the next dawn.

Attunement: Yes

Gloves of the Unraveled

Type: Wondrous item (gloves)

Description: These gloves constantly shift in color and texture, seemingly not fully present in reality.

Properties: While wearing these gloves, you can use an action to phase through solid objects as if under the effect of the 'Passwall' spell for up to 1 minute. This ability recharges after a long rest.

Attunement: Yes

Iron Conclave Sigil

Type: Wondrous item

Description: This small iron sigil is stamped with the symbol of the Iron Conclave.

Properties: While you carry the sigil, you have advantage on all Charisma (Persuasion) checks made to interact with members of the Iron Conclave.

Attunement: No

Rift Shard

Type: Wondrous Item

Description: The Rift Shard is a fragment of pure magical energy from the epicenter of The Shattering. It's an irregularly shaped crystal that pulses with a radiant light, illuminating an array of vibrant colors. It hums softly, resonating with the heartbeat of the world's magic. The Rift Shard is 6 inches in length and weighs 4 pounds.

Properties:

Magic Resurgence: As an action, a spellcaster holding the Rift Shard can channel its raw power to fuel their magic. When they cast a spell, they can choose to use the Shard's energy in place of their own spell slots. Using the Shard in this way uses a number of charges equal to the level of the spell cast.

Arcane Erasure: In the event of total magic eradication, the Shard can be shattered as an action, causing a massive release of anti-magic energy. This event would be cataclysmic, akin to a second Shattering, but rather than releasing wild magic, it extinguishes all magic within a vast radius. This action destroys the Shard.

Attunement: Yes, by a creature capable of casting at least one spell.

The Rift Shard has 20 charges and regains 1d6 + 4 expended charges daily at dawn. If you expend the Shard's last charge, roll a d20. On a 1, the Shard shatters, releasing a burst of raw magic.

Spells

Spells

Shatter Spark

School: Evocation

Level: Cantrip

Casting Time: 1 action

Range: 60 feet

Components: V, S

Duration: Instantaneous

Description: You hurl a spark of raw, unstable magic at a creature or object within range. Make a ranged spell attack against the target. On a hit, the target takes 1d8 force damage. The spell's damage increases by 1d8 when you reach 5th level (2d8), 11th level (3d8), and 17th level (4d8).

Rift Blink

School: Conjuration

Level: 1st

Casting Time: 1 bonus action

Range: Self

Components: V

Duration: Instantaneous

Description: The chaotic energy within you allows for brief teleportation. You teleport up to 30 feet to an unoccupied space that you can see.

Shape Matter

School: Transmutation

Level: 2nd

Casting Time: 1 action

Range: 60 feet

Components: V, S

Duration: Concentration, up to 10 minutes

Description: You reshape nonmagical material within a 10-foot cube you can see, creating simple shapes or crude objects.

Energy Cascade

School: Evocation

Level: 3rd

Casting Time: 1 action

Range: 150 feet

Components: V, S

Duration: Instantaneous

Description: You release a wave of raw magic that flows over the battlefield. Each creature in a 20-foot radius sphere centered on a point you choose within range must make a Dexterity saving throw. A target takes 5d6 force damage on a failed save, or half as much damage on a successful one.

Reform

School: Transmutation

Level: 5th

Casting Time: 1 minute

Range: Touch

Components: V, S

Duration: Instantaneous

Description: You can mend a larger object or even reform a completely destroyed one. The reformed object is structurally weak and prone to collapse. The following are limitations of the spell:

Object Size: The spell can only mend or reform objects up to a 10-foot cube in size. Larger objects or structures will require multiple castings of the spell.

Material Limitation: The spell can reform objects made of stone, wood, metal, glass, or similar inanimate material. It cannot reform objects made of magical materials, or those that are enchanted or cursed.

Fragility: The reformed object is structurally weak and prone to collapse under any significant weight or force. It is not suitable for usage in combat, load-bearing construction, or any other stressful situation.

Original Components: The spell requires at least 50% of the original material present within a 10-foot radius of the casting. If a significant amount of the original material is missing, the spell will fail.

Complexity: The spell cannot recreate complex mechanisms or intricate designs in the reformed object. Any such features in the original object will be lost.

Disintegration: The spell cannot reform objects that have been disintegrated or otherwise destroyed at a molecular level.

Chaotic Shield

School: Abjuration

Level: 6th

Casting Time: 1 action

Range: Self

Components: V, S

Duration: Concentration, up to 1 minute

Description: You create a swirling, unpredictable barrier of magical energy around yourself, absorbing incoming spells of 4th level or lower and occasionally reflecting them back at the caster. The spell has the following limitations:

Spell Absorption: This shield can automatically absorb any spell of 4th level or lower that is cast from outside the barrier, even if the spell is cast using a higher level spell slot. Spells of 5th level and higher are not absorbed and affect the barrier and its contents normally.Exclusion Area: The area within the barrier is excluded from area-effect spells of 4th level or lower. Such spells can still target creatures and objects within the barrier, but they have no effect on them. Area-effect spells of 5th level and higher affect the barrier and its contents normally.

Reflection: The shield has a chance to reflect absorbed spells back at the caster. This chance is equal to 10% per level of the absorbed spell. For example, a 4th-level spell has a 40% chance of being reflected. This reflection targets the original caster using the original spell attack roll or saving throw DC.

Single Target: The shield only protects the caster. It does not extend to other creatures or objects, even if they are being held or carried by the caster.

Movement Limitation: The caster's speed is halved while the Chaotic Shield is active. The shield requires intense concentration to maintain, limiting the caster's ability to maneuver quickly.

Concentration: The Chaotic Shield requires concentration to maintain. If the caster's concentration is broken, the shield immediately dissipates. The caster must make concentration checks as normal when taking damage.

Leviathan's Grasp

School: Conjuration

Level: 7th

Casting Time: 1 action

Range: 90 feet

Components: V, S

Duration: Concentration, up to 1 minute

Description: Calling upon the raw power of the ancient Arcane Leviathans, you cause spectral, ethereal tendrils to erupt from the ground within a 20 ft. radius centered on a point within range, creating difficult terrain and potentially grappling and restraining enemies in the area.

When a creature enters the affected area for the first time on a turn or starts its turn there, it must succeed on a Dexterity saving throw or take 10d6 force damage and be restrained by the tendrils until the spell ends. A creature that starts its turn in the area and is already restrained by the tendrils takes 10d6 force damage. A creature restrained by the tendrils can use its action to make a Strength or Dexterity check (its choice) against your spell save DC. On a success, it frees itself.

Rift Storm

School: Evocation

Level: 9th

Casting Time: 1 action

Range: 1 mile

Components: V, S

Duration: Concentration, up to 1 minute

Description: You raise your arms to the sky, invoking the raw, chaotic energies of the multiverse. A churning vortex of indescribable colors and sounds manifests above you, a mile wide, crackling with violent, destructive potential. As the spellcaster, you can designate a 60-foot radius circle within the range where the storm will concentrate its might.

Each round, at the start of your turn, the storm disgorges a number of energy bolts equal to 1d4. Each bolt randomly targets a creature or object in the area. The type of each bolt's energy is determined by rolling a 1d6 and consulting the following table:

- Fire
- Cold
- Lightning
- Acid
- Force
- Necrotic

Each bolt deals 2d10 damage of its energy type. Targets must make a Dexterity saving throw against your spell save DC. On a successful save, they take half damage.

You can maintain concentration on the Rift Storm for up to 1 minute. Every round that you maintain concentration, the storm continues to manifest energy bolts. As an action on your turn, you can redirect the storm to a different 60-foot radius within range.

Remember that maintaining concentration on this spell prevents you from casting other concentration spells, and any damage you take could potentially break your concentration. A vortex of chaotic energy is a terrifying sight, and can potentially affect NPC and creature morale.

Shatter Whisper

School: Evocation

Level: 3rd

Casting Time: 1 action

Range: 1 mile

Components: V, S

Duration: Concentration, up to 1 minute

Description: Your voice carries along the waves of unstable magic, allowing it to be heard by a specific creature you know within 1 mile. The targeted creature hears the message in its mind and can reply telepathically.

Echoes of the Shattered

School: Illusion

Level: 2nd

Casting Time: 1 action

Range: Self

Components: V, S

Duration: Concentration, up to 1 minute

Description: You project illusory duplicates of yourself that move with you, distracting your enemies. Attacks against you have disadvantage while the spell is active.

Mist of the Wandering Woods

School: Conjuration

Level: 2nd

Casting Time: 1 action

Range: 120 feet

Components: V, S

Duration: Concentration, up to 10 minutes

Description: You conjure a 30-foot-radius sphere of swirling mist reminiscent of the Wandering Woods centered on a point within range, heavily obscuring the area and making it difficult terrain for your enemies. When you cast this spell using a spell slot of 2nd level or higher, the radius of the fog increases by 30 feet for each slot level above 2nd.

Leviathan's Strength

School: Transmutation

Level: 4th

Casting Time: 1 action

Range: Touch

Components: V, S

Duration: 1 minute

Description: You channel the raw power of the Arcane Leviathans, granting a creature you touch advantage on Strength checks and saving throws, and additional damage equal to your spellcasting ability modifier on melee weapon attacks.

Nexus Pulse

School: Evocation

Level: 3rd

Casting Time: 1 action

Range: Self (15-foot radius)

Components: V, S

Duration: Instantaneous

Description: You release a burst of raw magic energy from a nexus point within you. Each creature within range must make a Constitution saving throw, taking 3d8 force damage on a failed save, or half as much damage on a successful one.

Shroud of the Unraveled

School: Illusion

Level: 3rd

Casting Time: 1 action

Range: Self

Components: V, S

Duration: Concentration, up to 1 minute

Description: You wrap yourself in an illusory distortion of reality, making yourself appear as if you were in a different nearby location. Attacks against you have disadvantage, and any creature that relies on sight to determine your location that rolls a successful attack on you has a 50% chance to miss. Roll a d6. On the result of a 4 or higher, the attack misses.

Non-Player Characters

Non-Player Characters

Iron Conclave

Commander Gaius Tarn: Gaius Tarn, once a decorated and revered general in the royal army, led his men to countless victories. He had a loving family and lived a content life, before the cataclysmic event known as The Shattering stripped him of everything. The magical fallout annihilated his home and took his beloved wife and two children from him. This tragic loss hardened Tarn, forging him into a relentless leader focused on eradicating the force that had torn his world apart: magic. As the commander of the Iron Conclave, he rallies his troops with passionate speeches, inspiring them with his strategic brilliance and personal vendetta against magic. Yet, he is a man teetering on the edge of sorrow and rage, driven by a past scarred with pain and loss.

Inquisitor Drava: Drava, an orphan born of The Shattering's chaos, found her purpose in the rigid order of the Iron Conclave. Raised within its ranks, she was molded into an expert magic hunter. Her cunning, ruthless efficiency, and unwavering loyalty saw her swiftly ascend the Conclave hierarchy, earning the feared title of Inquisitor. However, her ruthless demeanor hides deep scars, both physical and emotional. A brutal attack by a Resistance member left her with a facial scar and fueled her personal vendetta against magic users. To Drava, every captured mage is a step towards her vengeance.

Blacksmith Albern: Albern, once a jovial and respected blacksmith, found his life upturned when his son manifested unpredictable magical abilities following The Shattering. Fearful for his son's safety in a world that hunted magic, Albern made the difficult decision to join the Conclave. His warm heart belies his alignment with the Iron Conclave, and his smithy work for them is purely to protect his son. In the heart of the organization he aids, he dreams of a day when magic can be free again, and his son can live without fear.

Underground Resistance

Sorcerer Elandra: As a magic student at the Shattering's onset, Elandra barely survived the cataclysm. Horrified by the misuse of magic leading to such devastation, she pledged her life to restoring balance. Elandra is a bright light within the Resistance, leading with an unshakeable spirit and relentless optimism. Her goal is a world where magic can be a boon, not a curse, and she'll fight tirelessly to see it happen.

Therin the Swift: Raised in the slums, Therin found liberation in the shadows, honing his agility and stealth skills. When the Iron Conclave began its witch hunt against magic users following The Shattering, he felt a call to arms. As the Resistance's prime infiltrator, he uses his quick reflexes and wit to ensure the safety of magic users, navigating treacherous paths to smuggle them away from the Conclave's reach. His daring feats have made him a legendary figure amongst the Resistance.

Ancient Lirael: Before The Shattering, Lirael was a figure of power and wisdom, a revered Archmage known across the land. The Shattering stripped her of her magic, leaving her a mere shadow of her past glory. However, the knowledge and wisdom she retains have become invaluable assets for the Resistance. She mentors young, uncontrolled magic users, instilling them with discipline and control, and serves as a guiding beacon for the Resistance.

Neutral/Other NPCs

Ranger Yoren: As a guardian of the Wandering Woods, Yoren finds peace in the companionship of his animal allies and the solitude of nature. He observes the Iron Conclave's tyranny and the Resistance's defiance, preferring to remain a neutral entity in this conflict. He extends aid to both sides when necessary but values the tranquility of his woods above political warfare.

Curator Marvus: Obsessed with knowledge and history, Marvus retreated from society after The Shattering, dedicating himself to preserving the past within his expansive library. Eccentric and highly protective of his collection, he admits only those who prove their intellectual worth. His paranoia extends to anyone attempting to breach his sanctuary, but his thirst for knowledge is insatiable.

The Ghost of the Broken Spire: The Shattering's epicenter was once home to a powerful magic user, Quillara the Riftweaver, whose magical experiments went awry, causing the calamity. Now a spectral entity, she is bound to the ruins of her tower, reliving her failure that led to The Shattering. The ghost's interaction with the Characters can be capricious - she can be hostile, seeking vengeance for her state, or helpful, hoping to rectify the past by aiding those who could prevent another disaster.

Mazes

Mazes

Complex Maze

Complex Maze (solution)

Simple Maze

Simple Maze (solution)

Game within a Game

Game within a Game

Coin of Fates

Setup: Each player needs two coins of different values, representing the two forces in the New Dark Age: The Iron Conclave and the Underground Resistance. In the game, the higher value coin represents the Iron Conclave (due to their control and power), while the lower value coin represents the Underground Resistance (symbolizing their underdog status). A flat surface is required to play the game, and a line is drawn in the middle of this surface, dividing it into two halves.

Objective: The aim of the game is to get both your coins to land on the same side of the line, indicating the unification of forces or a significant shift in the power dynamic. The side (Iron Conclave or Underground Resistance) they land on can also be interpreted as who is gaining the upper hand in the conflict.

How to Play

Players take turns flicking both their coins towards the line from a set distance away.

After each player has flicked their coins, the round ends. The coins are left where they landed.

If both of a player's coins land on the same side, they score a point.

If a player's coins land on different sides, no points are scored.

After scoring, players collect their coins, and a new round begins.

The first player to reach a predetermined number of points (for example, 5) wins the game.

Additional rules and considerations

If a coin lands on the line, it is considered a 'Shattered Coin', signifying The Shattering event. It adds an element of unpredictability to the game, much like The Shattering in the world of New Dark Age. The round immediately ends, no points are scored, and a new round begins.

In a more complex version of the game, players can try to knock other players' coins to disrupt their score, adding an extra layer of strategy.

This game reflects the ongoing power struggle in the New Dark Age and the constant striving for alignment or victory. At the same time, it's a game of skill and chance, much like the circumstances in the world of the New Dark Age.

Food and Fuel

Food and Fuel

Shatterbeast Jerky (Snack)

Ingredients

- 1 lb beef (brisket or flank steak)
- 1/2 cup soy sauce
- 2 tablespoons honey
- 1 tablespoon cracked black pepper
- 1 teaspoon garlic powder
- 1 teaspoon onion powder

Instructions

Slice the beef into thin strips.

In a bowl, combine soy sauce, honey, black pepper, garlic powder, and onion powder. Add the beef strips and let them marinate for at least 6 hours, preferably overnight.

Dry the marinated beef strips in a dehydrator or a low-temperature oven (around 175°F or 80°C) for about 3-4 hours or until fully dried.

Let cool, then store in an airtight container.

Iron Conclave Stew (Meal)

Ingredients

- 1 lb beef chunks
- 2 tablespoons vegetable oil
- 1 onion, diced
- 2 cloves garlic, minced
- 4 carrots, chopped
- 3 potatoes, cubed
- 4 cups beef broth
- Salt and pepper to taste
- 2 tablespoons cornstarch mixed with 2 tablespoons cold water

Instructions

Heat the vegetable oil in a large pot over medium heat.

Brown the beef chunks on all sides, then remove from the pot.

In the same pot, sauté the onion and garlic until soft and fragrant.

Return the beef to the pot, add the carrots, potatoes, and beef broth. Season with salt and pepper.

Bring to a boil, then reduce heat and let simmer for about 2 hours, until the beef is tender.

Stir in the cornstarch-water mixture to thicken the stew. Simmer for another 10 minutes.

Serve hot, preferably with crusty bread on the side.

Underground Resistance Mushroom Soup (Meal)

Ingredients

- 1 lb assorted mushrooms, sliced
- 2 tablespoons butter
- 1 onion, diced
- 2 cloves garlic, minced
- 1 cup white wine
- 4 cups vegetable broth
- 1 cup heavy cream
- Salt and pepper to taste

Instructions

In a large pot, melt the butter over medium heat.

Sauté the mushrooms, onion, and garlic until the mushrooms are browned and the onions are soft.

Add the white wine and cook until most of it has evaporated.

Add the vegetable broth, then bring to a boil. Reduce heat and simmer for about 30 minutes.

Blend the soup using a stick blender until smooth (or to your preferred consistency).

Stir in the heavy cream, then season with salt and pepper.

Serve hot, garnished with fresh herbs or extra sautéed mushrooms.

Shattered Elixir (Non-Alcoholic Drink)

Ingredients

- 1 cup blueberry juice
- 1 cup sparkling water
- Ice cubes

- Fresh blueberries for garnish

Instructions

Fill a glass halfway with blueberry juice.

Add ice cubes, then top up the glass with sparkling water.

Garnish with fresh blueberries.

Serve chilled.

Rift Shard Cocktail (Alcoholic Drink)

Ingredients

- 1.5 oz vodka
- 0.5 oz blue curaçao
- 0.5 oz lemon juice
- 1 oz simple syrup
- Ice cubes
- Lemon wheel for garnish

Instructions

In a cocktail shaker, combine vodka, blue curaçao, lemon juice, and simple syrup.

Fill the shaker with ice, then shake until well combined.

Strain the cocktail into a chilled glass.

Garnish with a lemon wheel.

Serve immediately.

Remember to adjust these recipes to your taste and dietary requirements. Enjoy your "New Dark Age" themed feast!

Maps

Maps

The Broken Spire

The Undercity

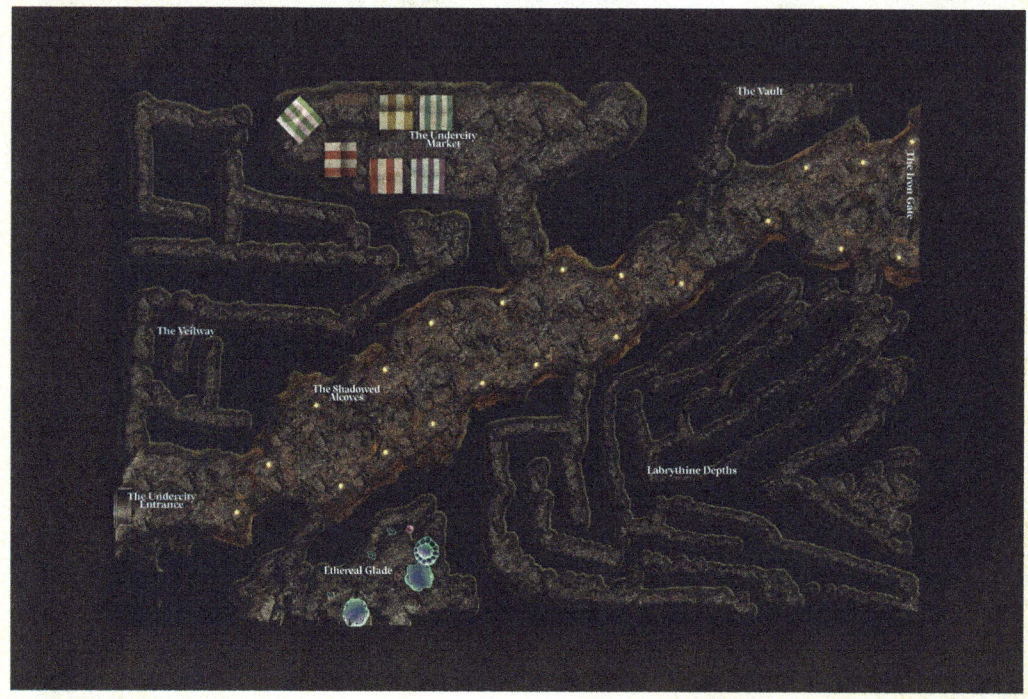

The Iron Conclave Fortress

Special Thanks

- Brian Fohlmeister
- Chris Sewell
- Captain Rik
- C. B. Pelton
- Christopher Milos
- David Stephenson
- didrik svahn
- Ed Bachner
- EposVox
- Fábio Balestro Floriano
- Graham Davey
- Henry Felschow
- Justing Offermann
- Len Krajewski
- Mark Flory
- Mariah Ward
- Michael G Shannon
- Michael T. Moon
- Scot Reed
- Sydney Wontor
- Oderus of Cthulhu
- Salvatore Puma
- Steve "El Guapo" Minogue
- Tyler Johnson
- Victor "Jako Dar" Morris

Credits

Author: M A D (aka, Matthew David)

Cover Art and Illustrations: Midjourney

Editor: Alysson Wyatt

Game Play Testing: Alysson & Martin Wyatt

PENNY BLOOD

BE THE HERO IN YOUR ADVENTURE

This work includes material taken from the System Reference Document 5.1 ("SRD 5.1") by Wizards of the Coast LLC and available at https://dnd.wizards.com/resources/systems-reference-document. The SRD 5.1 is licensed under the Creative Commons Attribution 4.0 International License available at https://creativecommons.org/licenses/by/4.0/legalcode.

Copyright © M A D / Matthew David / MAD Games 2023 - A Penny Blood Adventure

Made in the USA
Monee, IL
15 July 2023

38726723R10059